WITCH CAT

DEE'S MYSTERY SOLVERS

LEONARD D. HILLEY II

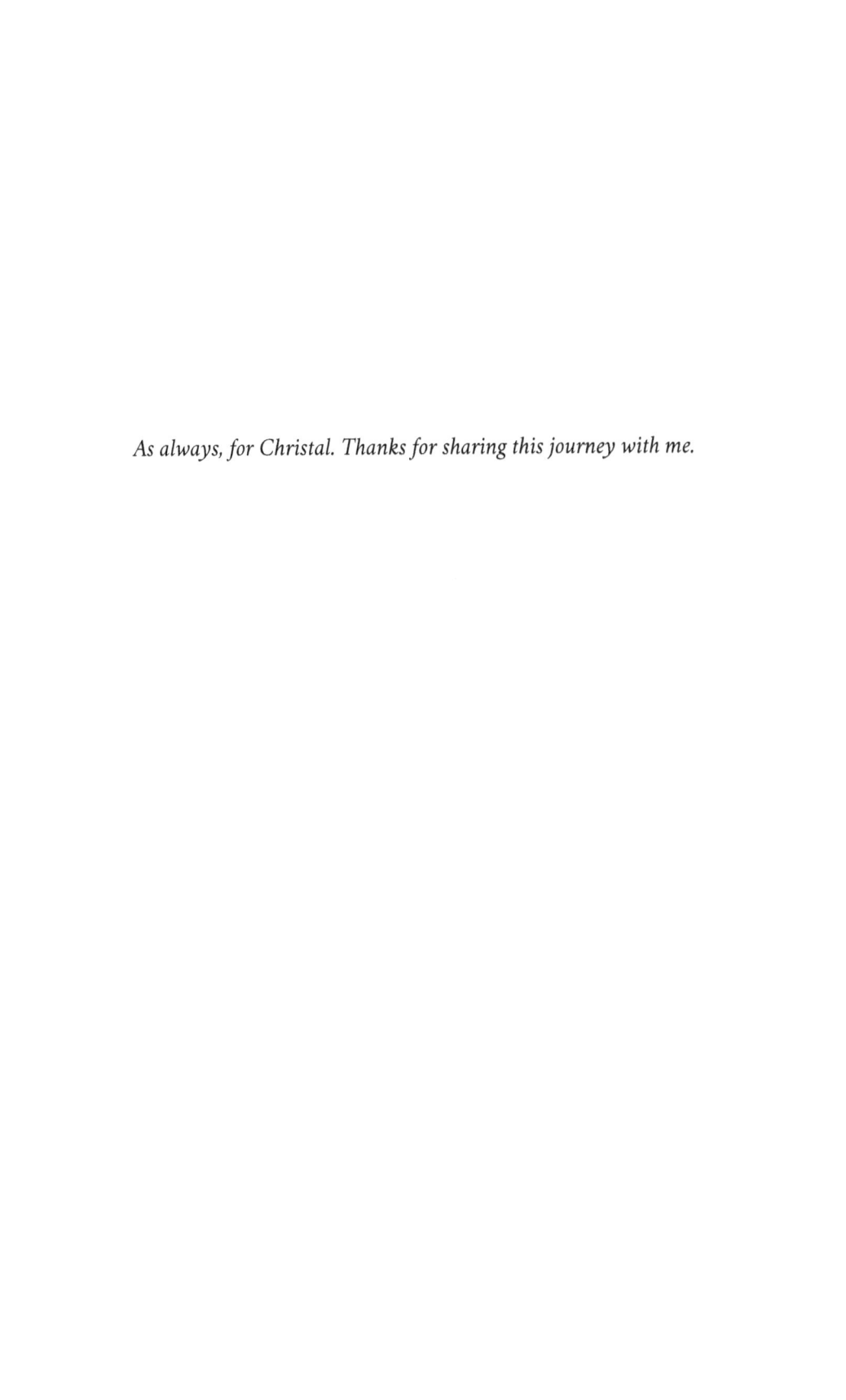

As always, for Christal. Thanks for sharing this journey with me.

INTRODUCTION

Saturday, June 12^{th,} Marty Sullivan's journal entry:

Since I'm the oldest member in Dee's Mystery Solvers Club, the other members probably think *I'm* the bravest, but ... no, I'm not. Dee, my younger sister, always brags to the rest of the club about how brave I am, but in reality, I'm far from it. If she only knew the truth, the *real* truth ... I'm afraid she'll think much less of me. I don't think she'd resort to calling me a sissy or chicken or anything like that, but she could never hide her disappointment. *That* would hurt worse than name-calling. But, my true fear is far greater.

My biggest fear is my biggest secret. I have kept this dark conundrum to myself. I don't know how Dee would react. Even now, I'm reluctant to write this in my journal because someone might find and read this.

Dee often jokes about how she wishes we'd encounter a *real* ghost, even though she knows the topic causes me discomfort. She says she's joking, but she really hopes we find one. The excitement in her voice and the gleam in her eyes indicates her true desire. I hope she *never* sees one. Why do I feel this way? Because *I* see ghosts. Quite frequently. To be honest, I wish I didn't see them. Ever since I found my mystical black cat, Edgar, in the haunted swamp on the outskirts of Tangled Forest, I've had the ability to see ghosts.

Maybe I didn't find Edgar. *He* found and adopted me to become his owner.

Edgar has the ability to materialize in some of the most unusual places. It doesn't matter where I'm at or how far I've traveled on my bicycle, he appears at my destination, almost instantly. But the truth be known, I never saw any ghosts until after I got Edgar. Edgar must be the link for why I have this ... weird ability. Too bad he can't talk. Perhaps he could better explain our connection to those who never crossed over.

Dee has scheduled a meeting for The Mystery Solvers to attend this morning. She always wants to solve mysteries. We all do. Today, I'll finally reveal my secret about seeing ghosts. Although, it might be best for me to hold my silence.

Dee will believe me. I have no doubt. Where will our adventures lead afterwards? I'm certain she'll demand a pursuit to find the true reason for why I'm cursed with this ability. She's not one to settle for mere speculation. She's too bullheaded to give up such a quest, which is why I've waited so long to reveal the truth. Brushing against the paranormal isn't as thrilling as she believes. But I'm tired of keeping this secret to myself. I want to know if there's any way I can stop it. Without losing Edgar, of course. He's the best cat anyone could ever ask for.

CHAPTER 1

Inside the Sullivan garage, Dee stood behind the wobbly old podium they had found outside the neighborhood church. Had they not taken it home, the podium was destined for the landfill after the trash service picked up the church's garbage.

Dee spared its early demise. Even though the podium lacked stability, it was usable for their club meetings. Standing behind it, she appeared more authoritative and gave her club leadership additional merit.

Dee exercised her authority by unnecessarily hammering her father's rubber mallet on the podium when she called their weekly meeting to order. The untidy garage was cramped and she could easily get her brother's and two friends' attention by clearing her throat.

Cardboard boxes from last summer's garage sale gathered dust and cluttered the floor and corners. They should've taken the unsold items to Goodwill, but no one wanted to bother packing the boxes and driving them to the drop off. Besides, Dee and Marty secretly wanted to keep some of their old toys their mother insisted they sell.

Dead silverfish carcasses caught in small spider webs meshed against the sides and in between the stacked boxes, old furniture, and discarded appliances. With their mother's fear of *any* spider, they didn't need to worry about her touching the boxes.

Various hammers, wrenches, and unfinished engine assembly projects cover Dee and Marty's father's worktable. His old rusty car set atop concrete blocks, without tires, and with its hood raised. Their father was a shade tree mechanic during his spare time. But lately, his job demanded far too many hours, out of state weekend business trips, and prevented him from working on the car. It was one of those *someday* projects he always talked about finishing.

The washer and dryer set against the corner wall near the door that led into the kitchen hallway. A soft scent of the lavender dryer sheets attempted to mask the oil and grease smells. The running dryer squeaked its protest for drying a heavy load of towels. Atop the dryer was a new belt their father had bought to replace the squeaky belt months ago. Their mother never openly questioned when he'd replace it. The old worn belt would probably break before he actually took the time to repair it.

Marty, Adam, and Lynn sat on the old beanbag chairs that remained unsold at the garage sale. Dee smiled at them, cleared her throat, and shook her head slightly. Her bobbed brown hair barely moved. She wore a green T-shirt and shorts with gray tennis shoes laced with bright neon green shoelaces. She rapped the mallet a couple more times on the podium. Seriousness narrowed her hazel eyes.

Marty shook his head. "Sis, you already have our full attention. Giving us a headache with the hammering isn't necessary. The squeaky dryer's bad enough."

Dee scowled. "First on the agenda. Lynn, how are the club badges coming along?"

"I've almost finished them." Lynn smiled with excitement. Her raven hair was pulled back in a neat ponytail. Her white powdered face was a direct contrast to her dark hair and almost black eyes. "Mom's going to sew the borders with her sewing machine."

"Great!" Dee said. "Having badges will help others identify our club whenever we're scouring the area, looking for clues. Okay, let's move on. *This* is our fourth meeting since we solved our great Halloween mystery by discovering the reason for the beating heart sound under Hollow Hill Cemetery. Since winter was too cold and snowy, we couldn't investigate any new cases. But it's summer now! Any suggestions for a *new* mystery we could solve?" She pointed at Lynn. "Lynn? You got anything?"

Lynn shook her head. "No mysteries, other than *why* we keep holding our meetings in your junky ol' garage. That squeaky dryer's gnawing my nerves."

Dee nodded and sighed. "I know. We need to find a clubhouse with more privacy and well, less clutter."

"One where we don't nearly trip with every step we take," Lynn said. "Or where we don't have to hold our breath because of filthy oil rags and gas fumes. In a strange way, the flowery dryer sheets makes it worse."

"I know." Dee sighed. She looked around the garage with disappointment. "We need a better place. A clubhouse would be nice."

"Something dark and spooky," Lynn said with a slightly evil grin.

Dee smiled. "Yeah, *that* would definitely be a great clubhouse. Others would be less likely to snoop around."

"Let's make that our objective today!" Adam tipped back his ball cap.

Dee crinkled her nose and shook her head. "Erm, not today. I'd rather find something more adventurous. Something spooky. So, Adam, have you heard of any unusual happenings in Ravenswood since school let out?"

"Nope. Sorry."

Dee sighed with slight frustration. "I really want a mystery to solve."

Re-ooow! Edgar mewed from the shelf directly behind Dee. She jumped, gave an abrupt scream, turned with a start, and gasped sharply.

"Where'd you come from?" Dee placed a hand over her heart. She turned toward her brother. "Marty, I swear your cat wasn't there a second ago. I'm certain I left him inside our house."

"You probably did." Marty grinned. "He has a way of . . . just showing up."

"How does he keep doing that?" she asked. "He did the same thing on Halloween. Even miles away from here, he suddenly appeared."

Marty nervously looked around at Lynn, Adam, and then he glanced at Dee. He crossed his arms. His brown eyes revealed that he wanted to talk, but he was holding back.

"What is it?" Dee arched a skeptical brow.

"What do you mean?"

Dee shrugged. "I know that *look*. You're itching to tell us something, or you're fighting the urge to tell us. Which is it?"

"Both. But . . ."

"But what?" Lynn asked. "You should go ahead and tell us. Perhaps we should vote on it?"

"That's not necessary," Marty said.

"How many of us want Marty to tell us?" Dee raised her hand and grinned mischievously.

Lynn and Adam raised their hands.

Marty grimaced. "I'm afraid you'll make fun of me."

Adam gave Marty a side-glance and shook his head. "We'd never do that. You're older than the rest of us, and you always have interesting things to discuss. We learn a lot from hanging around you."

"Thanks. I appreciate that."

"It's true," Adam said. "You're like a big brother to me."

"Can I ask you something?" Dee asked.

"What?" Marty replied.

"Where'd you get Edgar? You've had him for over a year, but you never told any of us where you found him."

"Well," Marty said. "Edgar's part of what I wanted to talk to you about. But he's not what you'll make fun of me about."

Dee stepped aside from the podium and motioned him beside her. "Take the floor and tell us. We won't laugh, I promise. Right, guys?"

Adam and Lynn nodded.

Marty stood with a sheepish look on his face. Though older, he didn't hide his anxiety. He stepped behind the rocky podium. Resting his hands on top of it, the pole wobbled. "What should I tell you first? Where I found Edgar or what I'm most afraid to discuss."

"Which is more important?" Dee asked.

Lynn took her pen and started writing their discussion into their meeting journal.

"I suppose they're about equal. However, Edgar might be the reason for the other matter," Marty said.

"Then tell us where you got Edgar first." Adam pulled the bill of his hat down.

Dee and Lynn nodded.

"Okay." Nervously, Marty propped his elbows atop the podium and leaned on it. "Last summer I rode my bike out to Tangled Forest."

Dee frowned. "Tangled Forest! And you didn't take *me*? That place is supposed to be haunted."

"You should've taken all of us," Adam said. "That would've been so cool."

Lynn grinned. "Wouldn't it have been?"

"We didn't have a club then," Marty said.

"So?" Dee gave him a shrewd grin. "I might've started our club a lot *earlier* if we'd all gone together."

Marty sighed and shook his head. "Okay, anyways, when I got to the Tangled Forest, a cat mewed deeper in the woods. Since there aren't any forest trails to ride my bike, I hid it behind a heavy curtain of thick ivy vines."

"I doubt anyone would've stolen it," Adam said. "Everyone knows those woods are haunted, and no one ever stops there."

"Did you see any ghosts?" Dee teased.

"Please, just let me finish telling you what happened." Marty's eyes narrowed and his nervousness vanished.

"Sorry," Dee and Adam said in a unified whisper.

"Thank you," Marty said. "Edgar cried, as if it was in pain, so I ran into the forest to find him. Well, I *tried* to run, but the thick vines and thorny briars slowed me quite a bit. Eventually, I reached an old church in the swamps."

Dee, Lynn, and Adam sat wide-eyed.

"You actually went *into* the swamp?" Dee asked softly.

Lynn said, "There's a church out there?"

Marty nodded. "Yes."

Lynn glanced at Dee. "I've never heard of an old church in those woods. Have you?"

"No," Dee said.

Adam shook his head.

"That's where I found Edgar," Marty said.

"Was he hurt?"

"No. He was stranded on a small island of moss in the cemetery beside a tilted angel tombstone."

"That cat couldn't possibly get stranded," Dee said. "He appears anywhere he chooses."

"I know, but he refused to leave the mossy mound. He acted like he wanted me to *rescue* him. Remember the heavy rain we had for three days and Ravenswood flooded? I found Edgar the day after."

"I remember the flooding." Lynn stopped writing and patted more white powder on her pale face. "I'm thankful we all live on the higher end of town."

They exchanged glances and nodded.

Lynn put away her powder brush and frowned. "The church has a cemetery in the swamp?"

"Yes."

"No one's ever mentioned a church or a cemetery. Not even Papaw."

"I know. It's rundown and seems to be forgotten," Marty replied. "Almost ghostlike itself."

"It's doubtful anyone's ever walked that far into those woods," Adam said.

"Not for decades, I'd say," Marty said softly.

"We have a mystery to solve." Dee grinned and her eyes widened.

Marty rolled his eyes. "I figured you'd say that."

"The situation deserves our investigation, right? Since there's a graveyard beside the church, the church's probably haunted. Probably why no one *ever* goes into that forest." Dee smiled. "Okay, you've explained how you found Edgar. What's your other secret?"

Marty took a deep breath, exhaled slowly, and then he swallowed hard. His face became a bit paler. He nervously made eye contact with Lynn, then Adam, and finally his gaze locked with Dee's. He said, "Ever since I took Edgar home, I—I've been able to see ghosts."

"No way!" Dee gasped. Her small hands balled into fists. Her face reddened. "You *know* I've always wanted to see ghosts! Don't you dare joke like that."

"I'm not joking." Marty's troubled eyes seemed haunted as his mind raced.

Dee rose slightly forward on the beanbag chair, pushed herself to her knees, and leaned closer. "You *are* serious?"

Marty nodded.

"You've seen ghosts?" Dee asked. "I mean, *real* ghosts?"

"Yes."

"When was the last time?" Adam asked.

"On Halloween night."

"This past Halloween? Really?" Dee asked.

Marty nodded.

"Why didn't you tell me? You know—"

"Dee, being able to see ghosts isn't as exciting as you think. Some of these ghosts . . . are *not* friendly."

"I don't expect you'd see Casper," Adam said with a wide grin.

Dee and Lynn giggled.

"You see!" Marty pointed a stern finger. "*That's* why I didn't want to say anything. The jokes."

"I'm not making fun of you. Honest." Adam straightened in his seat and waved his hands in surrender. "I'm sorry."

Marty shrugged and looked at Dee. "Some ghosts are vicious and vile. They won't attack people who can't see them, but once they realize someone sees them, they become aggressive and try to hurt you."

"Ghosts have attacked you?" Lynn looked up from polishing her nails with a fresh coat of black polish.

"Yes. Once an angered ghost chased me. I was lucky to escape."

Adam stood. "They're invisible spirits, right? How could they possibly hurt you?"

Marty turned and lifted the back of his tank top. A long white mark ran from his left shoulder blade across to his right one. "They might be invisible, but somehow, one slashed me."

"Dang." Dee came closer to inspect the scar. "Where'd you run into that ghost?"

"Old Lady Maggie's house. She hired me to clean the junk out of her attic."

"Seriously?" Dee asked.

Marty nodded.

Lynn looked at Dee. "I always thought *she* was scary."

"Not as frightening as the ghost in her attic. Do you see why I get nervous when you mention ghosts?" he asked.

"Yes." Dee nodded. "Okay, let me understand this correctly. You never saw any ghosts until *after* you got Edgar?"

"That's right."

Excitement widened her eyes again. She turned to the others and grinned. "You know what this means?"

"What?" Adam and Lynn asked.

Marty crossed his arms and waited for her answer. "Go ahead, Sis, say it."

"*We have a new mystery to solve!* We're going in the forest to find out why Edgar was there. Perhaps, we'll find clues to figure out why you can see ghosts."

No." Marty shook his head. "We're *not* going to Tangled Forest. Believe me. It's far too dangerous. That's why I've never gone back."

With great enthusiasm, Dee said, "Perhaps you need to go back. Maybe Edgar called you deep into those woods to help someone else. There must be a connection between the cat, the swamp, and your ability to see ghosts."

Marty shoved his hands inside his pockets. "I'm certain there is, but it's not a pressing issue."

Adam said, "Has Edgar ever tried to lead you back to Tangled Forest?"

"No," Marty replied. "And I've purposely never biked that direction since."

"Why not?" Adam asked.

"I'd rather not say."

"What if you returned? What do you think Edgar would do?" Lynn asked.

Marty stood silent and thought for several seconds. "I don't want to know."

"Why not? Marty, aren't you the least bit curious?" Dee asked.

"Of course I am, but what if he runs away and I never see him again? Besides, the dangers outweigh the good in finding the answer."

Adam turned his ball cap to the side. "Yo, we laugh in da face of danger."

Marty glared at him. "Always the cutup. You saw my scar. It was painful. Ignoring such dangers makes you vulnerable. I was lucky the injury wasn't worse."

"You're right." Adam straightened his hat and looked away.

"I know I'm right." Marty's face softened. "Look, I'm sorry for losing my cool, but none of you are taking this seriously, like I expected."

Dee returned to the podium. She rapped the top lightly with the mallet. "Okay, let's bring it to a vote. How many want to go to the Tangled Forest to find out why Marty can see ghosts?"

Adam and Lynn raised their hands. Marty crossed his arms and shook his head. Dee lifted her hand. "Three to one in favor. One opposed. So, *this* is our next mystery to solve."

"Just like that?" Marty frowned. "The three of you want to go in spite of my warning?"

They all nodded.

"Sure," Adam said. "We're curious as to what you've seen."

"Curiosity kills more than cats," Marty said.

Edgar mewed.

Dee placed her hands over Edgar's ears. "Don't listen to him, Edgar."

"What if I refuse to go?" Marty asked.

Adam's eyes widened with worry.

Dee scrunched her nose and offered a snide smile. "We'll go without you."

Her smile indicated she knew Marty would never let them go to the forest without him. Since he was the oldest, he was expected to keep them out of trouble and protect them. That was how a good older brother behaved. He and Dee's parents counted on him to do so.

If he knowingly let them wander into the forest and their parents found out, he'd be held responsible, regardless if anyone was hurt or not. The angered expression on Marty's face disappeared. He looked worried and concerned. A fraction of fear came to his eyes. Dee was stubborn enough to lead the others to the forest.

"Let's get our bicycles," Dee said. "Marty, when you found Edgar, did you see any ghosts in the swamp or woods?"

"No." Marty shook his head, grabbed his bike, and rolled it to the side door of the garage. "Not in the swamp. I saw ghosts only *after* I went to get my bike near the road. I noticed smoky images drifting through the trees."

"How many ghosts did you see?" Adam's former bravery diminished. "Were there a lot of them?"

"Two."

"Did they try to hurt you?" Lynn asked.

Marty shook his head. "No, they just drifted around. Of course, I didn't stick around to find out. Seeing the first two ghosts scared me enough that I never wanted to return."

"Have you ever wondered *why* Edgar was in the swamp?" Dee leaned and scratched behind Edgar's ears while balancing her bike with her other hand.

Marty nodded. "All the time."

Dee smiled. "It's apparent he has some kind of magical abilities since he seems to disappear and reappear at will. And you're certain you never saw a ghost nearby?"

"If Edgar's the reason I'm able to see ghosts, the ability probably hadn't settled over me until after I carried him back through the woods."

Dee smiled. "I've a good feeling we'll find out the reason why you can see ghosts then."

Marty grabbed his bike's handlebars. "As long as none of us gets hurt, it would be nice to know, but I don't want to lose Edgar."

Dee pushed her bike onto the driveway. Marty followed. Lynn and Adam ran across the street to their houses to get their bikes. The ride to the forest would take at least two hours. The walk through the woods to the old church in the swamps could take much longer, depending on what they discovered and how rugged the terrain was. If nothing went wrong, they hoped to be back home before sunset.

CHAPTER 2

*T*angled Forest was at the far end of the county, miles away from the Ravenswood community, and the distance was tiring for even the most experienced bicyclists on a hot June day.

At least a lot of the narrow, winding backwood roads were covered by leafy branches to block the summer heat. With the light afternoon breeze, the air was much cooler and pleasant.

Marty rode ahead of the group as they descended a steep hill. He took his hands off the handlebars and held them outward, allowing the breeze to rush around him. He closed his eyes for a moment, enjoying the whistling air and trying to suspend his worry about what they might encounter when they entered the forest.

He opened his eyes near the bottom of the hill. To the right side of the road was Ol' Henry's Grocery, a small store that sold basic odds and ends, along with bread, milk, and eggs for the locals who didn't want to drive all the way to Ravenswood. The old store was more than a hundred years old with Henry's father running it before passing it to Henry.

Marty glanced over his shoulder. "Did anyone bring a canteen?"

Dee shook her head. "In all the excitement, I never thought to get one."

"Nope!" Adam's voice was ragged. He huffed for air and sweat dripped down his flushed face.

Marty coasted into the gravel parking lot. "Let's buy some drinks, rest, and cool off. It's too hot outside, and we still have a ways to go."

"Great idea," Dee said. "I'm parched!"

They parked their bikes near the door, set the kickstands, and wiped the sweat off their brows.

"Couldn't we have picked a cooler day to do this?" Lynn eyed Dee and sighed. Lynn's black mascara ran like dark tears and streaked down her white-powdered face. She looked like a possessed clown from a haunted carnival or what some might picture a banshee to resemble.

Marty opened the store's door and old bells rattled on the inside of the glass. He let the others enter before him. Dozens of small buckets on crude wooden shelves were filled with various candies and gum. Coolers, illuminated by narrow backlights, hummed near the back of the room. Various soda brand placards were fastened above each door. An odd scent of tobacco mixed with solvents filled the air. Overhead fans squeaked and attempted to lessen the thick heat with their slight breeze.

Henry sat in an old rocker next to the cashier counter. He grinned at the four Mystery Solvers heading to the coolers to get drinks. Slowly, he stood and leaned against the countertop. His silver hair was thin, sparse. Despite his wrinkles and stooped posture, his eyes were bright and his smile was more mischievous than a ten-year-old boy who was up to no good.

Marty was the first to grab a soda and return to the counter.

"Marty and Dee?" Henry laughed. "What brings you kids so far from home? Your Pop know you're so far from home?"

Marty was taken back by the question. He avoided direct eye contact and studied the buckets of candy. "Ah, we're out riding around. Much hotter than we expected."

Henry laughed. "The Devil opened his furnace today."

Marty grinned. "Can't argue with that."

Henry scratched the side of his head. "School's already out for the summer, eh?"

"Yes, sir," Marty said.

"Year's flying by." Henry shook his head slightly and chuckled. His shaky voice crackled when he spoke. "Used to be when I was a young'un, we'd already be working the corn fields and tending to rows of mater plants from the time the sun peeked over the trees. Then we'd earn extra money loading hay bales onto wagon beds. You kids have it made nowadays."

Marty nodded. "Our Papaw says the same thing."

Henry chuckled. "Ah, he'd know, too. Life didn't have all the luxuries it does nowadays."

Adam and Lynn brought their drinks and stood behind Marty.

"So Marty," Henry said, "you never said why all of you are way out here in the country, miles from home. Roads are much too narrow and curvy to safely ride bikes out 'ere the way people drive their cars. Once upon a time folks obeyed traffic laws, red lights, and stop signs, but no more, I'm afraid. Ain't much reason for you to be riding bikes in this heat. No easy way to fix a flat, should you have one."

"We're going to Tangled Forest," Adam said.

Marty turned with a harsh stare.

Adam audibly swallowed.

"Tangled Forest?" Henry frowned and his scolding voice deepened. "You kids know those woods are haunted. Why would you think about venturing out there?"

Dee placed her bottle of soda on the counter and smiled. "We've got mysteries to solve, Ol' Henry."

"Mysteries, eh?" Henry shook his head and pointed a crooked finger at the door. "Now, lookie here. Those woods are a trifle dangerous and there've been folks who've gone in, but ain't never come out."

"For real?" Adam asked.

Henry adjusted his glasses and punched the prices of the sodas into his old cash register. "Plain as I'm a standing 'ere, son. Some spooky things have occurred out there. Take an old man's advice and get on your bikes and go home. I imagine your parents would skin ya alive if they knew you planned to go into those woods."

Lynn took several dollars from her back pocket to pool with the others to pay for their drinks. "So you believe there are ghosts out there?"

Henry's jaw tightened. His eyes grew grim. "Ghosts, goblins, evil sprites, and all sorts of creatures call those woods home."

Adam shook his head, glanced at Marty, and attempted to look brave. "The next thing you know, he'll be telling us Bigfoot is real."

Henry took a deep breath, straightened as best he could, and pointed a stern finger at Adam. "Don't you be making light of ol' Bigfoot now."

Lynn took her drink and twisted the top off. "You think Bigfoot's in those woods?"

"Not in *those* woods, I imagine," Henry said, scratching his brow. "Place is too spooky for him. But I know for a fact they do exist in the thick rainforests in the Northwest part of the United States."

"You've seen him?" Dee asked.

Henry shook his head. "No, but I heard one. A couple of them, I suppose, while we were camping. A living nightmare I ain't ever forgotten."

"What happened?" Adam asked.

"They's out there making all sorts of commotion with fierce growls deeper than an angered lion and they's a snapping all sorts of trees in half. We didn't sleep a wink that night, but we were too scared to peek out our tents. When the morning came, we packed up our gear and left."

Dee snickered. "Aw, you're just trying to scare us."

"And with good reason," Henry replied. "Cause what I told you is the truth. I swear upon my Mama's grave, and that isn't something I take lightly."

Adam took a slow sip of his soda before he said, "Bigfoot's real? What else? The Mothman? Godzilla?"

Henry gave Adam a stern stare. "Son, there are things in this world we might not understand, but that doesn't mean they don't exist. Of course there's no Godzilla, but some of those other things you don't think exist ... you'd be surprised to know the truth. Now, you'd be fortunate if ol' Bigfoot was what prowled Tangled Forest."

"Why's that?" Marty asked.

"Cause what's out in them woods is far, far worse."

Dee grinned. "Yeah, and for as long as I can remember, we were told the same thing about the beating heart under the cemetery, which turned out to be false."

"Ah, yes," Henry said. "Dee's Mystery Solvers got to the bottom of that case. I remember reading that in the newspaper. I had myself a good laugh when I read it. But, not really much of a mystery to solve, young lady."

Dee's face contorted from a mixture of anger and slight hurt.

Noticing Dee, Lynn asked, "Why do you say that, Mr. Henry?"

Henry chuckled. "Because all of us old folks told that story just to scare you kids enough to keep you away from the cemetery."

"You mean you knew *what* caused the beating heart noise?" Dee asked with a gaped mouth.

Henry nodded.

"Papaw knew, too?"

"'fraid so."

Adam glanced at Dee's disappointed face. Angered, he said, "If all of you lied about the beating heart, you're lying about the Tangled Forest, too."

"No, son, I'm not," Henry said. "Things out there in the middle of those trees ... let's just say many brave men have lost their gumption. We made up the tale for the cemetery, because ... well, you saw how the ground was collapsing all over the place with sinkholes. The last thing any of us want is for any of our children or grandchildren to be injured or die. Sometimes it isn't enough to tell a young'un to stay away from an unsafe place. Adding fear to a situation is far more convincing."

"Like Tangled Forest?" Dee grabbed her drink and squeezed it tightly in her clenched hands. "More trumped up tales to scare us and keep us from exploring."

"No," Henry said, sadly, in a pleading voice. "What I said is the truth, just like my Bigfoot encounter. Those aren't tall-tales or lies. They're not made up stories."

Dee shook her head. "Momma read us lots of fables and stories when we were little. A lot of those had lessons for us to learn. Moral of the story. One of my favorite ones was about a boy who cried, 'Wolf!' And how people eventually don't believe someone who keeps telling them lies."

"Look 'ere, young lady," Henry said with a stern voice. "I won't have you accuse me of such, when I'm telling you the truth. I admit the cemetery was a lie since you're older and have better sense. But—"

"Perhaps it's a lesson we need to learn for ourselves," Adam said. "Right, Dee?"

She gave a firm nod. "We faced our fears on Halloween night with the beating heart in the cemetery. I'm sure we can face others at Tangled Forest. Nothing out there is going to scare us."

"Perhaps not." Henry took the phone off its cradle attached to the wall. "But I do know someone who can scare you. How about if I call your father and grandfather and tell them that you're up to no good and where you are planning to go? And the two of you, what do you think your parents will do? A good hide-tanning is what all of you'd get, I reckon."

Dee, Adam, and Lynn paled.

Marty held his hands up in surrender. "That won't be necessary, sir. We'll go home. *Please* don't call our parents."

Henry studied their worried faces for several long seconds before slowly setting the phone back into its cradle. "That's better. As long as you head home, and I'll be watching you from the door to make certain you *don't* go the wrong direction."

"Come on, guys." Marty opened the door. He glanced at Henry. "Thanks for not calling our folks."

"Don't give me reason to, son. You're all good kids and I've known your parents since the time they's your age. Now be good and return home."

"Yes, sir," Marty said, nodding his head. After the others were outside, Marty eased the door closed behind him.

CHAPTER 3

"*W*hat are we doing?" Dee asked after Marty grabbed his bike and rolled it to the edge of the road. "We're *not* going home, are we?"

"Shh!" Marty whispered. "Of course we're not going home, even though we probably should. I don't want Henry to call our parents or Papaw, and we can't be certain that he won't anyway. So, let's head in the direction of our homes and sneak around a different way."

Adam rolled his bike to the edge of the road and eyed the steep hill they had descended. He sighed in disgust. "That means we have to pedal up the mountain of a hill?"

Lynn snickered.

Marty nodded. "Regardless, we have to eventually bike to the top again anyway. Once we reach the top, we'll take a side road and circle around where Henry won't see us."

Adam shook his head. Sweat beaded his forehead beneath his ball cap. "My legs are already tired and shaky. They'll be too sore for me to ride anywhere farther from home. I'll be lucky to even get home by the time we get to the top."

Marty grinned. "Suck it up. We're not even halfway to the forest."

Lynn groaned. "What?"

Marty shrugged slightly. "It's true."

Dee frowned with frustration. Tears shimmered in her eyes.

"You okay, Sis?" Marty asked.

She swung her leg over her bike. "I'm irked because they all knew what the beating heart was all that time. It wasn't even a real mystery. We never discovered anything."

"For us, it was a mystery," Adam said, "and *we* solved it."

"It's not the same thing," she replied.

"Isn't it?" Adam replied with a broad grin.

Dee's lips tightened. "I imagine Henry and the others got a kick out of reading about our solved mystery in the newspaper. Bet they laughed a lot."

Marty frowned. "Maybe. But Sis, you know what? Since we let everyone else know what made the beating heart sound, they can't use the story to scare other kids anymore."

A slight smile tugged Dee's lips. "You know ... you're right. Thanks. Now, let's go prove them wrong about the Tangled Forest."

"Uh, Sis—"

Adam started peddling up the steep hill.

"I don't think Henry was lying to us about the forest being haunted." Lynn used a handkerchief to wipe her running makeup.

"I guess we'll see," Dee whispered.

Re-o-ow.

Edgar sat on the gravel parking lot.

"Edgar?" Marty glanced at the cat.

"See?" Dee said. "He's the best sign we could get. Since you found him there, he wants to return."

Marty scooped up the cat and scratched behind its ears. "Nonsense. You know he was bound to pop up anyway, so his presence isn't a *sign* for us to do anything."

Dee laughed and pointed. "Looks like Adam's going to pass out before he gets halfway up the hill. Let's catch him."

Marty set the cat down and glanced to the door of the shop. "Yeah, we'd best hurry. Ol' Henry's still watching us."

Lynn and Dee pedaled ahead. Marty waved and smiled at Henry before riding after them.

"I can't believe he threatened to call our parents," Dee said.

"You think he would've?" Lynn asked.

"Most likely he'd have called Papaw," Marty replied. "He and Papaw grew up together. They're still great friends. I've no doubt he'd call Papaw in a second. While you *pretend* you're not afraid of what's in the forest, I'm pretty certain you don't want to see Papaw when he's angry."

Dee stood on the pedals to give herself more power to pull the steep hill. "You're right about the one thing but not the other."

"What do you mean?" Marty asked.

"Oh, I'm terribly afraid whenever Papaw or Momma get mad at me, but I'm *not* pretending that I'm not afraid of those woods," Dee replied. "Cause I'm not."

"Dee, some fears are in our best interests," Marty said. "It's what helps us make the right decisions so we know when to flee. Fear is more important than looking for a sign when one isn't there."

"I was only kidding about that. I'm determined to get to the bottom of what's going on there. If nothing else, I'll prove I'm not falling for any more tricks."

"Well, if you're looking for signs of whether we should explore the forest or not, perhaps the fact that Henry was a few seconds from calling our folks is a clear indication for us to go home and forget about the old church in the swamps."

"Not a chance, big brother," Dee replied. "Look, I've already told you before, if you don't want to go, we'll go without you."

"Not me," Lynn said. She smiled at Marty. "Not without Marty. And I'm quite certain Adam would rather go home with Marty and I than to follow you. He'd take any excuse to head home."

Dee frowned. Her jaw tightened. "Then I'll go alone."

Lynn's eyes widened.

Marty sighed. "You know I can't let you do that."

Dee grinned and her eyes brightened. "That's what I'm counting on."

"Consider this, Dee," Marty said. "There's a great chance one of us might get severely injured. How would that make you feel?"

Her grin faded. "We'll be careful. *Extra* careful."

"How can you be careful when you can't see the things I do?"

"You'll look out for us."

"I can only watch one direction at a time. I can see them, but I don't have any way to protect any of us against a sinister ghost, including me. As far as I know you can't destroy a ghost."

"Another reason *why* we need to find out how you got this ability," Dee said. "You didn't have it before you found Edgar, so the forest or the swamp holds the answer. It must. Race you to the top."

She stepped hard on the pedals, trying to pull the hill faster, but Marty clicked the gear control on his bike and passed her with ease.

"Hey!" Dee said. "No fair!"

Marty laughed and soon made his way past Adam. A few minutes later, he parked his bike at the side of the road at the top of the hill and waited for them.

CHAPTER 4

*M*arty sat balanced on his bike while he waited for the others to reach him.

Adam panted and pushed his bike to the side of the road. He didn't bother to set the kickstand and instead, he allowed the bike to fall into the grassy ditch. "I love going *down* the steep hills, but I *hate* pedaling up them. I can't wait until I'm old enough to drive a car."

"You'll miss riding these hills," Marty replied.

Adam shook his head. "Not so much."

Dee and Lynn pushed their bikes to the side of the road. Lynn had practically wiped all her makeup off, which only revealed that her skin was almost as pale without the layer of white powder she wore.

"Did anyone bring sunscreen?" Marty asked. "Lynn's going to get sunburned before we get to Tangled Woods."

"I have some in my backpack!" Dee smiled, unzipped her pack, and sorted through its contents.

Adam leaned and tried to look inside the pack. "What else you got in there?"

"A flashlight, matches, bandages, rope, twine, and other odd and ends," she replied.

"Prepared for almost anything, huh?" Lynn asked.

"We have to be," Dee replied.

"Except a canteen." Adam sneered.

"Yep," Marty said. "Look. Let's go home and try this again on another day."

"Nonsense. We've come this far, so which way do we go now?" Dee asked. Streams of sweat meandered her cheeks.

Marty's slightly narrowed gaze displayed his silent objection. "About a half mile ahead, there's an old dirt road."

"That's not a main roadway. It cuts through Farmer Tucker's pastures," Adam said.

Marty shrugged. "He won't care as long as we don't stop and bother his fruit trees."

"Are you sure?" Lynn asked.

Dee nodded. "Sure. Mom buys bushels of apples from him every fall to make homemade applesauce and apple butter, so he knows us."

"Don't talk about food," Lynn said. "I'm getting hungry."

"You should've bought food at the store," Adam said.

"I didn't bring enough money," she replied.

"Here." Dee reached into the pack.

"A granola bar?"

Dee offered a sheepish smile. "It's all I have."

"How old is it?"

"Last summer, I suppose."

Lynn scrunched her nose. "Ew, I'll pass." Her stomach growled. "For now."

"See, Dee?" Marty said.

"Nice poetry," Adam said with a slight chuckle.

Marty gave Adam a quick frown. Adam looked away. Marty faced his sister. "Dee, we should go home and plan this exploration tomorrow. We aren't fully prepared. We could leave earlier in the morning, when it's not so hot. I promise not to welch on it."

"How far are we from the forest?" Dee asked.

Lynn took out her cellphone and brought up a map. "Another forty-five minutes would be my guess."

Dee glanced at her wristwatch. "We've already ridden about an hour and twenty minutes. We're so close, Marty. Why turn around now?"

Marty sighed. "Look, I don't feel comfortable about going to the woods today. We have no real food. Henry saw us, and he could call our parents to make certain we made it home."

Dee frowned. "Fine. Let's take a vote."

"I vote we stop wasting time and you two stop arguing." Adam tugged the bill of his ball cap. "It's hot out here and Lynn's skin is turning pinker in spite of the sunscreen. We could've already been much closer to the forest if you two stopped fussing."

Marty nodded. "You're right. Sorry. Since we're this close, we'll ride to the forest. But, Dee, you need to make me a promise."

"What's that?"

"If I see something, something bad … we turn around and hightail it home."

"You mean ghosts?" Dee asked.

"Not just ghosts. But evil ones. Any like the one that left the scar on my back. Deal?" He held his hand out.

Dee studied his hand for a moment and looked into his eyes. She shook his hand. "Deal."

"Good," Marty said. "Let's go."

Re-oow.

Everyone turned to see the cat sitting behind them.

"Come here, Edgar," Dee said. "You can ride in the basket on my handlebars."

The cat scampered to her. She picked him up, patted his head, and placed him in the basket. "Come on, guys. If we hurry, we can probably reach the forest in thirty minutes."

Adam pushed his bike and began pedaling. "I don't think I'm that ambitious. My energy's gone."

"Granola bar?" Dee asked, extending one toward him.

"Nah," Adam replied. "Not yet."

They rode a half mile until they reached the farm. The narrow rode that cut through the farmer's orchard was compacted red clay and fairly even. Due to the heat and lack of rain, small plumes of red dust spewed behind their tires. They rode four abreast to keep the dust from sticking to their sweaty skin. A cool breeze flowed through the trees and offered the slightest relief from the overbearing sun.

Midway across Farmer Tucker's farm, two dogs yipped and barked as they rushed from the farmhouse toward them. Without further prompting, the Mystery Solvers increased their speed to keep distance from the excited dogs. The dogs didn't sound angry but one never knew when a dog's temperament could quickly change whenever strangers crossed their property.

After several minutes of chasing the bikes through the red dusty clouds, the dogs slowed and scampered off the side of the road and through the shade of the apple trees. Even the dogs seemed to think the heat was too much.

At the end of the red road, they came to the blacktop. Since this area of the county was rural, traffic remained sparse. A brown sign at the side of the road indicated it was two miles until they reached Tangled Forest.

Dee smiled. "Almost there."

"Thank goodness," Lynn sighed.

THE STATE OWNED THE FOREST, but due to the longstanding rumor that the woods were haunted, the town never invested any money to build park trails, campsites, playground equipment, or pavilions for visitors. Because of all the strange events that often occurred in Ravenswood, most of the townspeople were too superstitious to dare investigate the area. Every local person had heard about at least one horrific occurrence in the forest. Though no actual evidence was ever presented, few seldom asked for more details. Superstitions were powerful to adults as they were to children. Even Henry painted convincing details about Tangled Forest to send shivers down Dee's spine.

Few people were skeptical enough to question or explore the forest due to the overwhelming amount of dread associated with the mysteries of what lie inside the forbidden forest. Except, of course,

Marty. He decided it was worth braving his fears to save a cat, but Edgar wasn't an ordinary cat.

However, Dee was always more different than he when it came to the unknown. Marty often wished she was more fearful, but she challenged other people's superstitions. She sought evidence to prove or disprove whether monsters and ghosts were the culprits for the bizarre phenomenons. This was why she viewed herself as an investigator. More than anything else, she wanted their club to gain the recognition she believed it deserved.

She admired Marty for being brave enough to tell the group about his special ability, but she was also envious. She truly wished she could see ghosts. Although she wasn't certain *why* she'd like to see them, their quest into the swamps where Marty found Edgar might explain why he could see ghosts. Secretly, she hoped she might find a way to share that ability with him.

Tall towering trees stood along each side of the road and offered generous cool shade. While the four of them coasted in single file, Dee sped up to pull alongside Marty. Dee slowed her bike. Her eyes indicated she was lost deep in thought.

"What is it?" Marty asked.

"Have you ever wondered why ghosts are stuck on Earth after the person has died?"

"From time to time," he replied.

"Why do they linger?" she asked.

"Beats me," Marty said.

"Unfinished business?" Adam asked.

Dee thought for a moment and smiled. "That's a big possibility."

"Maybe they need to right a wrong or seek revenge against someone who treated them badly in life?" Lynn said.

"Another good point," Dee said. "We need to find out for certain."

Marty frowned. "How do you propose we do that?"

She laughed. "You tell us. You can see them."

"So?" Marty said.

Lynn rode alongside Dee and Marty. She glanced at Marty. "You showed us the scar from the ghost that attacked you. Haven't you ever spoken to one of the ghosts?"

Marty shook his head. "No. After the one attacked me, I'm not fond of getting close enough to *talk* to one."

"Do you think you will once we get where you found Edgar?"

Marty's eyes showed his uneasiness. "I don't know. I'll tell you if I see one."

Dee scratched Edgar beneath his chin. The cat closed its eyes and tilted its head upward, enjoying the attention.

"I wonder how Edgar will react once we get there?" Lynn asked.

"That'll be interesting," Dee said.

Marty stared ahead on the road. "I hope I don't lose him because we've brought him back."

"Why would he leave you?" Lynn asked.

"I'm more worried that someone or something will *take* him away from me." He pointed at the wide patch of gravel at the edge of the road ahead. A large crude sign with faint letters signified they were at the Tangled Forest. "We made it."

CHAPTER 5

*M*arty grinned at Dee when she swung off her bicycle.

Dee rolled her bike to the edge of the woods. "Where should we hide our bikes?"

A car slowed at the curve of the road where they stood balancing their bikes on the gravels. The elderly driver gave them an odd expression before she sped away. The bizarre look in her eyes seemed to indicate she must've thought they were ghosts, not teenagers.

After the car was out of sight, Marty said, "Last time, I hid my bike in the thick ivy behind those trees."

Adam frowned. "Shouldn't we keep our bikes with us in case we need to ride away quickly?"

"Look at the forest." Marty pointed. "Do you see any clear paths we can push them through?"

Adam studied the thick trees surrounded by thorny briars and thick underbrush. "No."

"Even if we need to grab them in a hurry, the vines covering the bikes won't slow us down. It's highly unlikely for anyone to stop if they spot them."

Dee nodded and grinned. "True. Did you see the horror on that woman's face when she saw us? She was so spooked, she wouldn't have slowed down to see if we needed help."

"Everyone believes these woods are haunted," Adam said. His nervous eyes stared into the shadowed trees.

Marty glanced at the road and then back at the trees. He nodded. "Regardless of what happens next, we're on our own if we need help."

"We have our cellphones." Lynn took hers from her back pocket and looked at the screen. Her eyebrows rose. "No signal?"

"We can't get any reception out here," Marty replied.

Adam audibly gulped. "That means ... we're in the *dead* zone?"

"Dun-dun-dun," Dee said in a deep voice. Then she laughed. "What's gotten into you, Adam? Are you getting nervous?"

Adam frowned and crossed his arms, trying to look braver. "No."

Marty sighed. "Come on, let's hide our bikes and go find the old church. I don't want to be here any longer than we need to be, especially *not* after dark."

Dee glanced at her watch. "We have almost three hours of daylight."

"Yes." Marty nodded. "But the trip home is about two hours and the farther we hike into the trees, the darker it becomes. I imagine it'll take about a half hour to find the church and possibly that long to return to our bikes."

"Where'd the time go?" Lynn asked, looking confused.

"It took a lot longer to get here than we planned," Dee said.

"Stopping at the store and the brief bickering took a chunk of our time," Adam said.

"Well, the more we stand outside the forest," Dee said, "the more time we're wasting."

"I agree, Sis." Marty yanked down a thick curtain of vines from the trees and with Adam's help, they covered the bikes.

"There," Marty said. "Even if someone walked past this spot, it's unlikely he'd see the bikes."

"Where's the best place to enter?" Dee stepped closer to the forest's edge. "Here?"

She pointed at a narrow path that was matted down from travel, but not from human feet. Possibly foxes, raccoons, deer, or some other animals used the path quite often. Briars and poison ivy kept the path partially covered.

"We can try it," Marty replied. "There aren't any true trails."

Adam looked at the path and then at Marty. "How'd you ever run through these woods?"

"It wasn't easy. The briars snagged my clothes and scratched me a lot," Marty replied. "To be honest, escaping the forest is a blur. I never felt any pain from the briars until after I stopped running."

Lynn slapped her arm. The harsh smack echoed. "Ugh! Mosquitoes!"

"I have insect repellant in my pack," Dee said.

"Good." Adam turned his hat around backwards. "Pass it around. I hate bug bites. I'll be itching all night."

Lynn sprayed her arms and legs with the insect repellant and handed the can to Adam. He quickly sprayed himself and returned the can to Dee.

"If you don't like itching, don't walk through any poison ivy." Marty pointed at the waxy, three-leafed vines clinging to the trees and creeping across the forest path. "Or you'll be scratching for days."

Dee and the others looked at the ivy and cringed.

Overhead, cicadas chummed in the trees. Katydids and crickets sang as well. Crows cawed deeper in the forest.

"Weird, isn't it?" Adam asked.

"What?" Marty said.

"Not any sounds of cars or trucks at all."

Marty nodded. "Exactly. That's why I said that we're on our own and why I'd rather have gone home today and come back better prepared tomorrow. Should anyone get hurt, we can't reach help quickly. So be extra careful and watch for snakes."

"Snakes?" Lynn looked nervously at her feet. "No one ever mentioned snakes."

Adam paled. "I never thought about them, either."

"I thought you laughed in the face of danger, Adam," Marty said.

"Not *all* dangers." His face was grim. His voice rose slightly and he gave a nervous smile.

"You don't have any choice in what dangers you encounter sometimes," Marty said.

"I'm starting to realize that," Adam said in a low voice.

"Me, too," Lynn said.

Dee sighed. "Are we going to wait until the sun goes down before we hike to the old church?"

"Uh, no-o-o," Adam said. "No, we're not. No way I'm setting foot in the woods after dark."

"I suppose you want me to lead the way?" Marty asked.

Dee shrugged. "You're the one who found the church and Edgar."

"This is your idea, Sis, not mine. Remember?" Marty frowned. "That's why I never wanted to tell you about where I got Edgar in the first place. I knew you'd want to investigate."

"Fine, I'll lead." Dee brushed past him and walked toward the narrow path.

"No." Marty rolled his eyes. Her bullheadedness annoyed him. "I'll go first. But again, for the record, I voted for us to go home."

"Noted," Dee said softly.

Marty stepped from the gravel into the forest. Pine needles and old leaves crunched underfoot. Immediately a briar snagged his sock, as though the briar deliberately reached out to grab him. Leaning down, he picked up a long stick and unfastened the briar. He used the stick to push aside the poison ivy vines while he walked.

"Wearing shorts wasn't a good idea," Dee said, glancing at Lynn.

"You're right," Lynn replied.

"The path only gets worse," Marty said. "So watch where you step."

FIFTEEN MINUTES of carefully working their way along the narrow path, their attention was more absorbed in avoiding the sharp thorns and the poison ivy than noticing the subtle changes of the surrounding forest. The vines and briars thinned, and soon no underbrush covered the forest floor. The ground became soggy. Where briars and poison ivy previously obstructed the path, now a thick soft carpet of green moss spread beneath their feet and through the dense rows of trees. Each step was cushioned with silence while they continued deeper into the forest.

Marty finally paused and looked around. The towering trees blocked the view of the sky and darkness crept around them. "We're getting closer to the swamp."

Lynn gasped.

"What?" Dee asked.

"This place is so different and dark. Kind of has a beauty I've never experienced, in a spooky sort of way."

Adam glanced at the tree canopy. "How long have we been out here? It looks like the sun has set."

Dee glanced at her watch. She tapped it with her finger. "My watch stopped working."

Simultaneously they checked their cellphones. With a nervous expression, she glanced at each of the others. "My cellphone isn't working."

"Mine, either," Lynn said.

"Did that happen before with you, Marty?" Dee asked.

"I don't know. I never checked my phone when I came through here."

"So we don't know what time it is?" Adam asked with wide eyes.

"No," Marty said. "But I don't think we've been out here a half hour yet."

"Yeah, but it's almost dark," Adam said.

"We can turn back," Marty said with slight hope in his voice.

Dee shook her head. "No. It only *looks* dark. We're not that far from the swamp, are we? With all this moss and the ground getting wetter, the swamp has to be nearby, right?"

"We probably are," Marty replied. "But, don't you think we're receiving plenty of significant warning that we shouldn't have come into the forest in the first place?"

Adam released a nervous chuckle. "This reminds me of one of

those cheesy horror movies where everything goes bad despite the growing threat."

"Yeah," Marty said, "but all the people in those films usually die."

"I know. Well, maybe that's not the best comparison."

"You think?" Marty shook his head.

Dee sighed. "Let's not sidetrack ourselves with negative thoughts, okay?"

Her voice was slightly shaky.

Adam gave her a shrewd grin. "Getting nervous, too, huh?"

"No," she replied firmly. "I never pictured the woods to look *quite* like this."

"I warned you," Marty said. He took a slow step forward and placed his left foot on a huge mossy log. "The place is creepy and why I had run out."

He adjusted his weight on his foot to step atop the log. The partially rotted wood cracked. A long black snake slithered from beneath the log and crawled away, resembling a fast moving black ribbon.

Lynn shrieked.

"It's just a black racer," Marty said. "Harmless."

Wide-eyed, Lynn frantically placed her hands across her chest and looked around the forest floor. "Where there's one snake, there's usually others."

Adam nodded. "That's what my dad says all the time."

"Well, that one can't hurt us." Marty stepped on the log and held his arms out to maintain his balance before jumping down. "All clear on this side. No more snakes."

"Have you seen any ghosts yet?" Dee asked.

"No, thankfully. But I'll tell you when I do."

"Good," she said. "We haven't seen Edgar in a while now."

"He might have gone home," Adam said.

"Unlikely," Dee said. "He's an explorer like the rest of us."

"Could be he's waiting for us in the swamp," Lynn said.

Marty offered his hand to help Dee down off the log and then to Lynn. "I guess we'll have to wait and see."

CHAPTER 6

The shadowed trees became even darker by the time they reached the swamp. Nature triumphed her glory with the songs of frogs, peepers, cicadas, and other insects and birds. The world outside this tranquil swamp didn't seem to exist.

Tiny floating islands of sphagnum moss protruded through the black shimmering pools of swamp water. Bent, dead saplings poked through the water like long, twisted fingers curled in death.

At the water's edge, the path divided into two narrow tracks. A rusted old wagon wheel was propped against a wide tree trunk and covered by a thick layer of moss. The wheel must have been over two hundred years old. A stack of rotted wooden crates rested a few feet away from the wheel, and were also forgotten by time long ago.

Marty and the others stopped at the faint trace of an old wagon trail. The chorus of nature across the swamp suddenly silenced. Curtains of Spanish moss swayed on the massive tree branches as an acrid gentle breeze flowed past.

Light flickered across the black water, shimmering only for a moment. The light was bright enough to grab their immediate attention.

"What's that light?" Adam whispered with slight fear.

"I don't know," Marty said. "I never saw anything like that when I was here before."

Dee pointed. "Is that the old church, Marty?"

Marty nodded.

"You crossed through the swampy water?" she asked.

"No. This path leads to the church and is fairly dry."

Re-e-oo-ow? Edgar's cry echoed in a questioning tone.

Dee looked at Marty. "Did you hear that?"

"Yes," Marty said. "It's Edgar. Do you see him?"

"No," Dee replied.

Lynn and Adam shook their heads.

Re-ee-o-o-w!

"Sounds like he's near the church," Lynn whispered.

Marty sighed. "I think you're right and that worries me. I hope I don't lose him."

"Come on," Dee said. "Let's go get him."

Another burst of light flashed and was gone in an instant.

"What is that?" Adam asked. "It's gleamed twice now."

"I've no idea," Marty replied. "But I see a ghost."

"Where?" Dee rose on her tiptoes and looked toward the church.

"Outside the church doors."

"Drat!" she said. "I don't see it."

"Me either," Lynn said. "Not that I expected to or even *want* to."

"But I *want* to see it," Dee said. "What's it look like, Marty?"

"Hard to say exactly from where we stand, but she's wearing a dress."

"Does she glow or pale? Transparent?" Dee asked.

"She's brighter than most ghosts I've seen," Marty replied. "Almost like pale glow of a yellow moon."

"What's she doing?" Adam asked.

"Standing at the door. Edgar's sitting at her feet, staring up at her."

"Do you think he belonged to her?" Dee asked.

"Possibly." A glum expression hung on his face. "Now I'm certain I can't get him back."

"Don't be so sure. Was she here before?"

"I didn't see her, but at the time I couldn't see ghosts, so maybe she was," Marty replied. "She could've been there the entire time and I didn't know it. If Edgar belongs to her, I'm certain she won't part with him. I know I don't want to."

Adam frowned. "You think Edgar's a ghost cat?"

"He's something paranormal," Marty said. "How else can you explain the way he appears out of nowhere, even when we're miles from home."

Dee offered a reassuring smile to her brother. "This is why we're here. To solve how he's capable of doing that."

"No, sis. That's the mystery *you* want to solve. I was content having Edgar as my pet. I accepted him for what he is, and I don't know need to know how he vanishes and reappears. Since we've brought him here, I might lose him."

"I'm sorry."

"Sorry's too late, sis."

Dee frowned with determination. "I'll go get him for you."

"You can't see the ghost," Marty said.

"No, but I see Edgar and that's enough."

Adam reached for Dee's arm but wasn't fast enough. Dee marched down the old wagon trail toward the old church with her gaze set on Edgar. Chill bumps prickled her arms since she couldn't see where the ghost was and didn't know what the ghost might do.

"Wait," Marty said.

Dee glanced over her shoulder but continued walking. "Do you want Edgar or not?"

"Of course, but from this distance I can't tell if the ghost is hostile or not."

"You said they only attack those who see them. I only see Edgar."

"I don't know if that's completely true or not. If Edgar actually belongs to her, she might become violent," Marty said.

Dee shrugged. "I got us into this mess and since I'm the club's leader, it's my duty to make things right, brother."

Adam grabbed Lynn's hand. "Not without us. We voted to come, too."

Lynn gulped but nodded her nervous agreement.

"Besides," Adam said, walking past Marty with Lynn. "we're stronger as a group than we are separately. Right, Marty?"

"Yes."

A sense of relief claimed Adam's face. "So you're coming?"

"Yeah."

"Good," Adam said. "At least you can see what the ghost is doing."

Marty jogged to catch Dee. "Sis, let me up front in case this ghost is a bad one."

CHAPTER 7

*M*arty walked ahead of the others, a bit less apprehensive than he would've been had he come alone. Even though he was nervous, he fought hard not to show it for the sake of the others. Since he was the oldest, he had to protect them, which meant if things got nasty, he was the one to stand between them and the ghost. So he needed to look brave and hide his fear.

When the Mystery Solvers stood across a narrow pool of water encircling the churchyard like a castle moat, the ghost's attention turned from Edgar to them. Tendrils of gray fog slinked across the water's surface. The trees settled into deeper darkness. If he believed magic loomed over the swamp, he'd have thought the sudden changes in the terrain were meant to trap them. He no longer questioned the rumors of Tangled Forest being haunted. The swampy forest held a mysticism and seemed to have a power of its own.

The ghost turned toward Marty and the others. Her transparent appearance reminded him of hologram images in sci-fi and fantasy movies. But no animators could capture the reality of this ghost on film. Holograms were cast shadows of what a person looked like and were harmless. Ghosts, however, could be quite dangerous, depending on their nature.

This ghost watched the Mystery Solvers and knew where they stood. They didn't have any way to hide without her locating them. As best he could tell the ghost didn't appear hostile but her true nature might be concealed to lure him closer. Her face held a troubled but curious expression as she studied them. But Marty's spectral attacker held a peaceful countenance moments before turning into a frenzied sinister spirit bent on inflicting pain. His scar proved how violent a ghost could be.

To the far side of the deteriorating church was an old small graveyard. Some gravestones were broken, sinking, or tilted. Atop one larger tombstone was a large cherub with chipped wings. The stone angel was angled and seemed destined to fall flat on its face. The swampy, moist soil prevented the heavier stones from retaining their necessary stability. The swamp was claiming everything, and eventually, nothing visible would remain to let the world know people had been buried here.

Few ever ventured into these woods and he'd never heard anyone mention the cemetery inside the haunted forest. Not even Papaw Sullivan. These graves and the memories of their existence were long forgotten, which was rare. How could families abandon their ancestors' graves? People seldom forgot their loved ones. Was this another reason to support the haunted forest theory?

The ghost raised her right hand and pointed directly at Marty.

"Marty," she whispered. "Please, come closer."

He looked at the dark water. The ground where he stood became wetter, miry, and the earth attempted to suck his feet downward. He couldn't stand where he was much longer anyway or he'd be unable to pull his feet free.

Apparently noticing his nervousness, Dee asked, "What's wrong?"

"She knows my name," he said softly.

Adam and Lynn gasped.

"What does she want?" Dee asked.

Marty took a deep breath and tried to remain brave. "She wants me to cross the water and come to her, but she hasn't told me why."

"You can't do that," Lynn whispered frantically.

"I mean you no harm," the ghost said.

Marty glanced at Dee. "She said she won't hurt me."

"Do you trust her?" Dee asked.

Lynn placed her hand on his left arm and squeezed. Her gaze was pleading. "Don't go to her."

Marty offered Lynn a brief smile. "If I want Edgar back, I have no choice."

"Be careful." Tears edged Lynn's eyes. The remnants of her mascara trickled down her cheeks.

"Yeah," Adam said. "We can't see her, so it's hard for us to help. Well, if we'd be any help at all against a ghost."

Marty stared at the water for a moment before jumping across. When he landed, his feet sank several inches in the moss-covered mud. He pulled one foot out and stepped higher on the bank where the ground was firmer. He walked closer to the ghost and Edgar, but kept what he believed was a safe distance in case he needed to run.

"Who are you?" Marty asked.

The ghost folded her hands together. She offered a slight smile and acted shy in answering his direct question. "Sara Wolcott. My name's on the gravestone over there."

Marty looked to where she pointed. The gravestone was nearly covered by the swamp water.

"Is she talking to you?" Adam asked.

Marty nodded.

"What does she look like?" Dee asked. "Ask her if we could see her, too."

Sara smiled. Her facial features were that of a young lady who had been attractive when alive. In a way, her beauty remained. Marty guessed she'd died early in life.

"Why can I see you and they can't?" Marty asked, ignoring Dee's question. "Ever since I found Edgar and took him home, I've been able to see ghosts. I don't understand why. Perhaps you can tell me?"

"It's a gift bestowed to you," Sara replied.

"I don't consider it a gift."

"But it is."

"Why do you say that?"

Sara smiled with patience. "Those of us who are trapped in-between this life and what lies afterwards need mediators."

"Mediators? You think I'm a mediator?" Marty frowned.

"If you choose to be," she said softly.

"How? I'm a teenager."

"Younger folks have more innocence. They're more receptive to spiritual things most adults shun. You must have a kind heart and a gentle mind. Otherwise, you'd never heard my cat's cry for help. Perhaps, you can help me pass to the afterlife?"

"I don't know anything about that," Marty said.

Dee crossed her arms. "Ask her to appear for all of us!"

Marty turned, frowned, and placed a finger to his lips. "Shh."

"She really wants to see a ghost, doesn't she?" Sara asked.

Marty rolled his eyes. "It's a *dream* of hers. She's jealous I can see ghosts. Why couldn't she be the one with this gift?"

"That wasn't my doing," Sara replied. "But since they're with you, I can appear for all of you to see me, but only for a few minutes. After I fade from their sight, you will still see me and other ghosts. They cannot."

Slowly, she materialized. Her skin glowed a yellowish tint. Her bonnet and long dress were several centuries old.

"I see her!" Dee said. She jumped across the water and ran to stand beside Marty. "Oh ... my ... gosh! You're a real ghost!"

Adam and Lynn gaped and exchanged glances. They glanced behind them. Realizing they were standing alone, they hurried to Marty and Dee.

Sara regarded Dee for a few moments. "At least one of us is happy about me being a ghost."

Dee's eyebrows rose. "Oh, I'm sorry. I—I didn't—"

Sara laughed softly. "It's okay. I died a long, long time ago, Dee."

"How do you know my name?"

"Edgar, as you call him, told me all about you and Marty. He's also mentioned Adam and Lynn and how the four of you investigate mysteries."

"Cat's can't talk," Adam said.

"Some might debate that," Sara said. "Cats can see and speak to the spirits of those who've passed on. Besides, cats have personalities, don't they?"

"Edgar certainly does," Marty said.

"Definitely," Dee said. "He sneaks up and frightens me all the time. Sometimes, I wonder if he doesn't like me."

"He likes you," Sara said. "But Marty is his favorite."

"Edgar makes that a bit obvious." Dee nodded and glanced at Marty with wide eyes. "Hey! How'd you know his name was Edgar?"

Marty shrugged.

"Actually," Sara said, "His true name is Pyewackett. He told me Marty had changed his name to Edgar, so—"

"Pyewackett? That's a cool name. I like that. What's your name?" Dee asked.

"Sara Wolcott."

"Why are you … here?" Lynn asked, unsuccessfully trying to comb her matted hair with her fingers.

"I'm stuck in this realm." Sara wrung her ghostly hands together. Sadness came to her eyes.

"You can't pass on?" Dee asked.

Sara shook her head. "Not yet. That's why I need your help."

"Our help?" Marty asked.

"Yes. You came to learn more about Edgar and why he's the way he is?" Sara asked.

"That was *my* suggestion," Dee said proudly, crossing her arms and giving a triumphant smile to Marty.

Marty rolled his eyes.

"It was my plan long before you thought to come here," Sara said.

"What do you mean?" Dee asked.

"Child, I've waited many decades for someone worthy of rescuing us. Marty could never have seen or heard Edgar if he didn't possess compassion," Sara said. "Edgar was stuck with me."

Edgar rubbed his head against the hem of Sara's skirt and purred.

"So he's a ghost, too?" Adam asked.

"Sort of," Sara said.

"Why can't you pass on?" Marty asked.

"Until I break the curse someone cast upon me when I was killed, I'm stuck between this world and the afterlife," Sara said.

"Why were you killed?" Dee asked.

"Because I was accused of being a witch."

CHAPTER 8

"*A* witch?" Dee asked with wide eyes. "Why would they accuse you of being a witch?"

Sara smiled. "Because I *am* a witch."

"Is this why you can't pass to the afterlife?" Lynn asked.

"No," Sara replied. "Witches can pass on, but my chief accuser was also a witch. He cursed and bound me to this patch of land outside the church."

"Why?" Dee asked.

"To prevent me from exposing his fraud against the tiny, prosperous town in these woods."

Adam glanced around. "There used to be a town here?"

Sara nodded. "This was Ravenwood's original settlement. Because he cursed me, the swamp is slowly being swallowing what's left of the town. I suppose somehow his curse spilled over to the rest of the town, too."

"Who was your accuser?" Dee asked.

"The pastor of this church."

The four Mystery Solvers' eyes widened from shock.

"The pastor?" Marty asked.

"Yes. He was a practicing witch, except he used black magic, which was something I never practiced."

Lynn asked, "Who was he?"

"Reverend Luther Chavies," she replied.

"He founded Ravenswood," Dee said with a gasp.

"He's regarded as an esteemed minister," Marty said. "There's a statue of him in town."

A soured expression claimed Sara's face.

"He was a witch?" Dee asked with a confused frown. "You're certain?"

"Yes. Six other women and I were hanged for being witches."

"How many witches lived in the old town?" Lynn asked.

"Of the seven women hanged, I was the *only* witch amongst them. Luther knew that, but he feared I'd tell others about his practice of the occult, which would forever tarnish his reputation."

Dee shook her head. "Why'd he do that?"

"He capitalized on the townsfolk's fears of the unknown. Being as this area was surrounded by dark forests where strange noises cried and echoed each night, he convinced them evil had somehow crept into our town. By convenience he lumped me into a group of women and accused us of being witches and ordered us to be put to death."

"If he knew the others weren't witches, why'd he want them dead?" Dee asked.

Sara sighed. "By making the townsfolk believe he was eliminating witches—the devil's associates—he made himself appear more holy and prominent in their eyes. He could claim how he had saved the town from evil and they'd hold him in higher esteem. It must've worked since the town has paid homage to him."

"Why didn't you protest and reveal his true nature before you were hanged?" Marty asked.

"I tried," Sara said. "I vowed to when he brought the constable to arrest me. But before I could reveal his plot and who he truly was, he cast a silence spell on me. I was unable to speak. I couldn't utter the slightest protest or make a sound. And until today, Edgar was the only one I could talk to."

"You can talk to us," Dee said with a smile. She glanced at Marty and the others. "Right, guys?"

Adam and Lynn nodded.

"You're so kind," Sara said. Gloom shadowed her gaze. "But, as I told Marty earlier, I'm only able to appear to the rest of you for a short time. After I fade, he's the only one who can still see me."

"You said you need my help," Marty said. "That I could be a … mediator?"

Sara nodded. "Yes. With your help, I can cross over."

"What do you need us to do?" Dee asked. "We'll do whatever we can to help you. Within reason, of course."

"The spell binding me here must be broken or I'm doomed to reside here forever."

"How do we break the spell?" Dee asked.

"Only one thing can break his spell, but I doubt you'll find it."

"What?" Adam asked.

"My silver bell. I always used it before I started my magical rituals," Sara replied.

"How will that break the spell?" Dee frowned.

"Reverend Chavies stole it after he silenced me. He knew if I rang the bell once, his spell would be broken. His negativity and control would be expunged. I could've summoned an Elemental or a Watcher to aid me and reverse his spell to silence him."

Dee walked toward the church. "Is the bell hidden around the church or is it underwater somewhere?"

Sara shook her head. "It's nowhere near me. I've searched the perimeters of the circle his cast and bound me to. When everyone fled this town, Reverend Chavies must've taken the bell to the new settlement."

Dee eyed the other Mystery Solvers. "It's not much to go on, but it's better than wasting time searching here. Sara, tomorrow, the four of us will search Ravenswood archives at the library and maybe the courthouse records. I promise we'll do everything we can to find the bell and bring it to you."

Sara smiled. "You're so gracious. I appreciate your help."

Dee nodded. "It doesn't mean we'll find anything useful, but hopefully, we will."

"I understand," Sara said. Her image began to fade. A slight haunted expression reflected in her dimming eyes. "You'd best hurry on your way out of the forest. After nightfall, more ghosts surface. Some aren't friendly at all. The bitter ones resent the living. They won't hesitate to attack you. So be on your way and good luck."

Sara's image grew fainter.

"Wait," Marty said. "What happens to Edgar after we find the bell and you break the spell? Will he cross over with you?"

Sara smiled. "He can stay with you, if he chooses. Since he's fond of you, and you've treated him well, I'm certain he'll remain with you. He's a free spirit to choose his own direction. Blessings to you, children. My time to be seen has come to an end except for you, Marty."

CHAPTER 9

*A*fter Sara's ghostly image faded, Dee looked at Marty. "Is she still there?"

Marty shook his head. "No, I don't see her."

"She said you'd still be able to see her."

"I know, but maybe she's tired?"

Adam said, "Do ghosts get tired?"

"Good question," Dee said, looking at Marty for the answer.

Marty shrugged. "I've no idea. But if you spent hundreds of years stuck in one place, wouldn't you tire of it?"

Dee frowned. "I never considered that. Imagine how horrible it'd be."

Lynn glanced at the darkening trees and the swamp. Odd birds squawked deeper in the forest where blacker shadows clung to the thick trees. "Guys, it's getting dark fast."

"We've been here longer than we should've stayed," Dee said. "Marty, we need to get our bikes and go home."

Marty rolled his eyes. "Really? You don't have to tell me. Had you listened to me, we'd already be home. Come on. If we're not home before 9 p.m., Dad's going to be steamed."

"Yep," Dee said with a sudden worried expression. "Mom will be even madder."

Marty winced.

Dee sighed. "We can't afford to be grounded, not when we need to find that bell."

The four hurried across the damp sphagnum pools.

"Where's the best place to begin our search tomorrow?" Lynn asked.

"I'd say the library," Dee said. "They have an archive room dedicated to the founding of Ravenswood. Perhaps, we can find more information about Reverend Chavies."

"That occurred over two hundred years ago," Adam said. "It's going to be impossible to find much helpful information and even harder to find Sara's silver bell."

"Ravenswood prides itself on its history," Dee said.

Lynn frowned. "But how much of it is reliable? If what Sara said about the reverend, most of the history will be false information."

"We always have the town's archived records," Dee said.

"They may not be accurate, either," Lynn said.

"True," Dee said.

"Shh, guys," Marty said. "Lower your voices. Can we discuss this *after* we're outside the forest?"

"Sure," Dee replied. "Why?"

"Ghosts are materializing in the forest and along the edge of the swamp," Marty said softly. "We can't afford for them to see or hear us."

"You see them?" Dee asked with slight optimism in her voice.

Marty gave her a stern look and nodded.

"Bad ghosts?" Lynn's eyes widened. Her pale skin made her appear almost spectral.

"I can't determine from this distance," Marty said. "I hope they're not, but the less attention we draw to ourselves, the better, okay?"

"My lips are sealed." Adam used his fingers and motioned like he was zipping his lips.

"Do you think the other ghosts are the reason Sara disappeared so even you couldn't see her, Marty?" Lynn asked.

Marty shrugged. "I guess that's possible. She seemed uncomfortable about nightfall, and *she's* a ghost herself."

"Can we hurry?" Lynn whispered.

"No faster than when we came this way. Well, maybe a tad quicker since we yanked most of the briars and ivy off the narrow trail. But watch where you step," Marty said. "In the darkness, it's hard to distinguish a snake from a stick."

"Marty! Why'd you have to say that?" Lynn searched the ground frantically.

Adam released a nervous chuckle and tried to get behind Marty on the trail.

"What do you think you're doing?" Dee said, preventing Adam from squeezing around her.

"Getting in front of you," he replied.

"Hey!" Dee said.

Marty glanced over his shoulder. "Let him, Sis. Everyone knows snakes generally bite the second person in line."

"What?" Adam said.

Marty nodded.

"Aw, now, you're making that up," Adam said. He glanced at Dee and while his head was turned, Marty gave her a wink. "Isn't he, Dee?"

"Yeah, he's making it up, Adam. By all means, please walk ahead of me." Dee stepped slightly aside to let Adam pass.

Adam stopped. After a couple of seconds, he swept his hand forward and said, "Nah, that's all right. Ladies first."

"Such chivalry, Adam." Dee scrunched her nose. "You put our ankles at risk rather than your own."

"Uh, well, someone needs to bring up the rear," Adam said.

Dee laughed. "Yeah, right."

Owls hooted. A whippoorwill repeated its endless chant. Had the Mystery Solvers not been in such a hurry to leave the forest, they might've taken the time to hear the humor of the birds' almost feuding banter.

"Whip-poor-will, whip-poor-will, whip-poor-will."

Followed by, "Who? Who? Who?"

"Whip-poor-will, whip-poor-will, whip-poor-will."

"Who? Who? Who?"

From the treetops a loud, nerve-grating screech echoed. A large object swooped downward.

Adam screamed.

Marty shushed him.

Large wings flapped. The huge owl flew over them and upward to perch in a tree.

"It's an owl." Marty shook his head at Adam. "For a moment, I thought Lynn had screamed. Didn't know you held such a high-pitched squeal."

In the fading daylight, Adam's blush was still evident. "Sorry."

BY THE TIME the Mystery Solvers reached their bikes and pulled them from the wilting curtain of vines, nightfall had settled over them. The asphalt was cooler, and a sticky dew was falling.

They managed to avoid the half dozen ghosts Marty had seen along the way, but jagged briars scraped their bare legs and arms. The shallow cuts ached when cool air brushed over them or when salty sweat ran over the injuries.

Frustrated, Marty yanked his bike and rolled it to the edge of the road. "This isn't good, Dee. We're miles from any streetlights. In a few minutes, it'll be pitch black, which will slow us down. We're already going to be late getting home."

"I'll take the blame for it," she replied.

"For all of us?" Marty swung his leg over his bike. "You know Dad will hold me responsible, not just for you, but for Adam and Lynn, too. It doesn't matter what kind of explanation you give, I'll be blamed because I'm the oldest."

"I'll talk to Dad, okay?"

"And tell him what, Sis? That we were exploring Tangled Forest?" Marty pedaled away.

Dee hopped on her bike and hurried after him. "I'll make something up."

Marty laughed and shook his head. "Sis, you've never been able to fib to Dad. He always sees through you. You can't hide your guilt, but I suppose that's a good thing."

"Wait up!" Adam rode behind them and almost bumped Dee's rear tire. "It's too dark. I can barely see your outlines. Where's your flashlight? One of us should hold so anyone driving a car will see us."

"Good idea," Dee said. "It's in the side pocket of my pack."

Adam rode closer, unzipped the pocket, and took out the flashlight. He fumbled with it and almost dropping it on the pavement. Finally, he clicked it on and aimed the beam to the road ahead of them. "It's not much, but it's a lot better than nothing at all."

"We'll be lucky if the batteries last until we reach the streetlights," Marty said.

"How about a little optimism, brother?" Dee said.

"Really, Sis? Optimism? I might've lost my cat for good because we went into the swamp. You want me to feel positive about it? I knew coming here was a bad idea. I knew it. We've no guarantee of finding the witch's bell to break the spell, and without it, I can't get Edgar back."

"It'll work out," Dee said softly.

"You don't know that. None of us do."

"Guys," Adam said. "There's a vehicle approaching."

The roar of an engine rumbled over the hill they were approaching. The headlights grew brighter and struck their eyes full force when the truck reached the top of the hill.

Marty and the others pulled to the edge of the road.

The truck stopped beside them and the window lowered. "There you kids are. Put those confounded bikes in the back of the truck and get your tails inside."

"Papaw?" Dee said.

"You know not to be this far from home after sunset. I ought to tan all your hides. Come on! Get yourselves in here, now!"

"Yes, sir," they said in unison.

CHAPTER 10

*D*ee and the Mystery Solvers sat in silence for about five minutes.

"Now, I don't know what possessed ya'll to be messing around in Tangled Forest, but I'm guessing it has to do with your mystery-solving group?"

"Yes, sir," Dee said.

"What exactly are you trying to solve?" he asked, not looking in their direction. The lights on the dash console made his wrinkled face seem contorted.

"Uh—" Adam said, before Dee elbowed his side.

"We can't say right now," Dee said.

"Ah, now, is that so?" Papaw said. "Confidential secret stuff, huh?"

"Yes."

"What about you, Marty? You want to tell me what the four of you were doing way out here?"

Marty glanced at Dee. Even in the faint light of the dash lights, her pleading eyes begged him to keep the secret. He sighed. "I can't right now."

"Can't or won't?"

Marty shook his head. "A little of both, Papaw."

"You realize how mad your father will become when he discovers you were at Tangled Forest, especially at this hour?"

"Yes, sir," Marty and Dee said.

Papaw chuckled. "I understand how a haunted forest entices young curious minds. But haunted or not, wandering off like this without letting me or your parents know where you are … that's just plain foolishness. There are dangerous things in them woods."

"Ol' man Henry told you we were out here, didn't he?" Dee asked.

"Ah, yeah, Henry gave me a call. Ol' man, huh? Henry and I are the same age. I guess that makes me an old man, too?" He glanced toward them.

None offered to agree or reply.

Papaw laughed harder. "Of course, I'm an old man, full of wisdom."

"How did Ol' Henry know we'd gone to the forest?" Dee asked. "We headed back the same way we'd come."

Papaw smiled. "Henry was a kid once. He half expected the four of you would find another route to the forest. When he called, he asked if I'd seen you or if you were home yet. When I asked him why, he told me you visited his store. I suspected where the four of you were headed. I had no other choice than to get out here and pick you up. It was almost dark when he called."

"Are you going to tell our parents we were at the forest?" Lynn asked.

"Well, I've been thinking that over. I really should, you know? Cause you being out this far from home after dark isn't safe," Papaw replied. "But, no, I'm not going to tell them, but if Henry hadn't clued me in as to where you were, your folks might've called the Sheriff's office. Your names and faces would be on the evening news, and the entire town would be looking for you. You don't want that type of exposure when you're in a secret club. Besides, how embarrassed would you be if your friends heard you were *lost* when you really weren't?"

"Ugh," Adam said. "They'd really laugh at us when school started in the fall."

Lynn nodded. "I get enough teasing about how I look."

"What do you mean?" Papaw asked.

"My makeup," she replied. "Zombie girl was going around this past year."

"Yeah, that doesn't sound too good," Papaw said.

"Are you kidding?" Lynn said. "Zombies are cool. There so *in* right now!"

"Until you wake up with one gnawing on your leg!" Papaw laughed.

"What?" Adam, Dee, and Lynn asked at the same time.

"Uh, nothing," Papaw replied. "Forget I said anything."

"So, Papaw, what are you going to tell our parents?" Marty asked.

"I'll tell them you've all helped pick green beans and tomatoes for me to take to the farmers market tomorrow," Papaw said.

"Thanks!" Adam said, relieved.

"Don't thank me yet," Papaw said. "Cause that's what you're going to do first thing tomorrow morning."

"Pa-a—paw!" Dee shook her head.

"It's either that, or I'm telling them where I picked you up. I won't straight out lie to them to cover your tails, and if you're picking vegetables tomorrow, it's not quite a lie. The way I see it, I'm doing you a favor. Having you pick the beans and tomatoes is your way of returning that favor. Besides, there are four of you, so it won't take you nearly as long as it would an *old man like myself*." He grinned and looked at them. "Do we have a deal?"

In glum unison, they replied, "Yes, sir."

"I expect all of you to be ready at sunrise before the day gets hot. No lollygagging, either. Understood?"

They nodded.

Papaw dropped Lynn off at her house first and then took Adam home. When he pulled into Marty and Dee's driveway, he turned off the ignition.

Marty opened the door and got out. "See you in the morning, Papaw."

"Sleep good. You're going to need the rest," Papaw replied. "The garden is loaded, so you have your work cut out for you."

Marty grinned. "Okay. Goodnight, Papaw."

After he sprinted up the driveway, Dee slid closer to the door and stared at the floorboard.

"What's wrong, Dee?"

With slight hurt in her eyes, she said, "Why'd you let me think I had solved a major mystery last Halloween?"

Papaw frowned. "What'cha getting at?"

"Ol' Henry told us that you and most all the adults knew what the beating sound really was and that I never solved a mystery at all."

"But you solved it for yourselves, right?"

"Yeah, but it's not the same. We were tricked into believing it was a heart and not what we found," Dee said softly.

"Don't be so glum. It took courage and wit to get to the bottom of the mystery."

"But you duped us," she replied.

Papaw rubbed his whiskered chin. "I suppose I did, but you also know why I did it."

"I guess so."

"Of course you do. It's because I care about all of you and that old cemetery is a dangerous place. I didn't want any of you falling into one of those sinkholes and getting hurt. Or worse, get yourselves killed. You're getting older, and you're a bit stubborn when it comes to finding out why certain things are the way they are. If I had to guess, I'd say Marty probably tried to talk you out of going to the forest. Right?"

Dee grinned. "Yes, Papaw, he did."

"But he went along to ensure none of you got hurt."

"Yes, sir."

Papaw laughed. "I don't know what exactly you're hoping to discover about Tangled Forest, but I want you to promise me something, okay?"

"What's that, Papaw?"

"Promise me that you'll always act on the right side of the law with your investigations."

Dee gave Papaw a side-glance. "I will."

A gentle smile crossed his face. "I know you say that and you probably mean it right now. But some mysteries might gnaw at you enough to make you do almost anything to solve it. You could be tempted to even bend or break a law or two to discover the truth. When you come to that place, you need to soul search and put that notion aside, okay?"

"Okay."

"All of you are good kids with bright futures ahead of you, so don't screw it up by getting into trouble."

"We won't."

"Ah, but today you went where you weren't supposed to be without letting us know. Don't ever do that again, okay? If something bad had happened, and one of you got severely injured, you can't get to a hospital on a bicycle. Certainly, not fast enough. Your cellphones don't work in that part of the county."

"I know. That's something we found out today," Dee said softly.

"See? That's why it's important to let us know. I could've told you there's no phone reception in that area. Now, go on and get some sleep. You have chores in the morning."

"Goodnight, Papaw, and thanks for picking us up."

"Any time, Sweetie."

CHAPTER 11

$\mathcal{T}$he four Mystery Solvers rode their bikes and arrived at Papaw's house before daybreak. He stood dressed in overalls and tossed cracked corn on the ground for his Rhode Island Red hens. The chickens bustled against one another, greedily scratching and pecking the corn off the loose soil.

Papaw glanced at his watch. "I'm impressed. Didn't expect all of you to actually rise this early on a Saturday. If you hurry with the picking, I can get the produce to the market by nine."

The high humidity made the thick air sticky and difficult to breath. The short bike ride to Papaw's farm had soaked their clothes with sweat. Their wet clothes clung to their skin. The grass was wet with heavy dew.

Adam left his bike on its side in the yard. He yawned, stretched, and watched the chickens peck the ground.

Lynn rubbed her eyes. Her pale face lacked any powder or mascara but even in the dim lighting, her skin looked like a porcelain doll's face.

Marty propped his bike against the outside barn wall. He walked inside the barn and came back a few minutes later with a stack of tall wooden bushel baskets. He set them on the ground, slid off the top basket for himself, and immediately headed toward the long rows of green beans.

"Four rows of green beans and four rows of maters," Marty said, eyeing the garden. "So we take a row of each."

Dee reluctantly grabbed the next basket and took the row of beans beside Marty's. She sighed and lowered to a crouch beside the green plants. She quickly plucked a handful of swollen green pods. After dropping them into the bushel basket, she wiped the dew off her hand onto the front of her shirt.

Lynn scooted to the row beside hers, so they could face one another and talk while they picked.

"It's going to be a long morning," Dee said.

"I know, right?" Lynn replied.

"Only if you let it." Marty grinned. His bushel basket was already a quarter filled with beans.

Adam turned his ball cap backwards and crouched at the last row of beans. He peered from where he sat to the far end of the row about thirty yards away. To anyone, the row seemed endless and hours worth of life-sapping work. He shook his head and snapped off the green pods one at a time with rebellious disdain. He didn't have to mention his inner agony of the toiling labor because his facial expressions detailed it all.

"None of us want to be here," Dee said. "Not when we really *need* to be researching Reverend Chavies to see if we can find Sara's silver bell."

"The longer you sit and pout, the longer we're going to be here," Marty said. "Picture the end of the row as the finish line. Once you're there, we pick the tomatoes and we're done. Just focus on one goal at a time. Beans, tomatoes, and then the library."

"Not without a shower," Dee said.

"Oh, definitely," Lynn said, "A shower and afterwards, I must apply my makeup."

Adam rolled his eyes. "Why must we pick the beans first?"

"They take the longest to pick," Marty said. "Unless you're quick like me."

Papaw finished feeding the chickens and walked to the edge of his huge garden. He tipped his straw hat back and used a red flannel handkerchief to wipe sweat from his brow. "I have a new twenty dollar bill for the one who finishes picking first."

Dee and Lynn perked up. They plucked the fattest pods as fast as possible and clunked them into their baskets.

"No way we're going to catch Marty!" Adam dropped to his knees and pulled off green beans.

"We all started at the same time," Marty said. "I'm just more enthusiastic about getting finished, so I can free up the rest of my day."

"Enthusiastic? Now, there's a word I don't think I've ever heard used to describe bean-picking before." Papaw laughed. "What are your plans today, Marty? You going fishing?"

Marty shook his head. "No, not today."

"Ah, I see. Do your plans have anything to do with Tangled Forest?"

Marty's eyes widened momentarily. He gave Dee a quick glance.

"Now, Papaw," Dee said, "I believe we made that perfectly clear last night. Secret club info."

"Eyes-only type of stuff, again, huh?" Papaw asked.

"Yes."

"Okay, then. I've got some other things to tend to, but I'll be back in time to see who claims my twenty dollars." He smiled and turned to walk away.

"Papaw?" Marty said, pausing from his picking.

"Yeah?" He looked back.

"Were you aware that Ravenswood was first settled *in* Tangled Forest?"

Papaw rubbed his scruffy chin and gave a slight nod. "I'm not much of a history buff, but according to the town monuments, this was recorded as the second settlement for Ravenswood. Why?"

"Just curious."

"Were you trying to locate the old homesteads?" Papaw asked.

"We were curious as to why they resettled here."

Papaw laughed. "I know I'm old, but that was long before my

parents were born. There are lots of books in the library about the origins of this town. You'd do good to check those out."

"That's what we want to do when we finish picking vegetables," Dee said. "It's good to know our town's history."

Papaw chuckled. "You might not want to learn too much. Lots of skeletons in the closets, even in the pioneer days. They say curiosity killed the cat, but it's really meant to dissuade people from putting their noses where they don't belong. So while you're trying to get to the bottom of whatever's gnawing at your minds, be aware to not dig too deeply. You might find answers you don't like."

"Your curiosity's never gotten the best of you, Papaw?" Marty asked.

Adam noticed Marty had stopped picking beans, so he doubled-down and picked faster, trying to catch up.

"My curiosity has *always* gotten the best of me," Papaw replied. "Still to this day."

"So you went into the forest?" Dee asked.

"Many years ago a couple of my friends went with me into the forest. We were kids about your age. Maybe a few years older. Henry was one who went into the forest with us. We didn't get too far. Strange spooky stuff goes on in those woods."

"Like what?" Marty asked.

"I honestly couldn't tell you. We all felt creepy inside, like we were being watched. It's a strange place, and I'm not the only one who'd tell you that, either."

Marty and Dee nodded. "We know."

"So you *did* go into those woods, didn't you?"

Dee said, "What I *mean* is a lot of people have told us the same thing."

Papaw eyed her sternly for several moments until Dee blushed and looked away and then he smiled. He glanced at Marty. "Where's your ol' cat? Usually I've tripped over him a half dozen times by now."

"I've not seen him today," Marty said.

"Humph. That's odd." Papaw walked to the carport at the side of the house.

After Papaw was out of earshot, Dee and Lynn stopped picking beans. Dee looked at Marty

"You haven't seen Edgar this morning?" Dee asked.

Marty shook his head and returned to plucking beans. "No. That's why I'm in a hurry to get this done."

"You think he stayed with the ghost?" Lynn asked.

"She's his rightful owner," Marty said. His eyes filled with determination and he hurried to finish his chores. "But if I want any hope to get him back, I have to finish this and find that bell."

Adam used both hands and yanked handfuls of beans off the plants. "I was hurrying to win the twenty dollars, but Marty, helping you get Edgar back is worth far more than the money."

"Thanks," Marty said.

Adam looked up long enough to show his broad smile. "That's what club brothers are for, right?"

Marty nodded. "Yep."

WHEN PAPAW RETURNED to the garden about an hour later, the four Mystery Solvers were carefully taking the large red tomatoes from the last few tomato plants. He shook his head. "I have to say that *this* is some kind of record performance. I figured the four of you would still be up to your ears in green beans. Kids these days don't usually have the work ethic like kids did when I was growing up. I'm proud of you."

Each of the four stood at the last tomato plant on his or her chosen row. With large red tomatoes in hand, they smiled and nodded at one another before pulling their last tomato at the exact same time.

"Unbelievable," Papaw said. "A four-way tie!"

They hefted their baskets of tomatoes and carried them out of the garden.

"Well, the reward was for twenty dollars, so I guess we need to have a tie-breaking event, huh?" Papaw asked.

"No," Marty said. "We can split it."

"Agreed, "Dee said. "We've got things to do."

Papaw reached into his back pocket and took out his wallet. He thumbed out three twenties. "Look, you guys did a fantastic job, so you split this up evenly. It'd be more except you *did* owe me a favor."

"Sixty bucks?" Dee said. "No, Papaw that's too much."

"No, kids, you've earned it. I expect today's gonna be a scorcher, so treat yourselves to an ice cream or milkshake later. Or, put it in your club till."

"That's a good idea," Dee said. "We've never discussed having a treasury for our club, which means we'll need to vote for a treasurer and then—"

"Dee, go enjoy some ice cream and discuss it with your club later," Papaw said. "I've got to get these bushel baskets loaded on my pickup."

"I'll help," Marty said.

"Me, too," Adam said.

CHAPTER 12

*a*fter the boys helped Papaw load the baskets of beans and tomatoes onto the truck, they watched Papaw drive away before grabbing their bikes.

"Here." Lynn unzipped her backpack. She reached inside and pulled out four identical patches. They were in the shape of a large red letter D with a lower case 's attached; each was outlined in silver. Behind the D's was the outline of a magnifying glass. Beneath the D's was 'Mystery Solvers' in bold black letters. "I finished these last night."

Dee took hers. Her mouth gaped. "Wow! Lynn, these are fantastic! Did you make these by yourself?"

"My mother helped me set up her embroidery machine, but other than that, yes. I did most of the work," Lynn replied with a red blush.

"These are great," Adam said.

"I love it!" Marty said with a broad smile. "Something I'll wear with pride."

Lynn reddened even more, and she quickly glanced away from Marty. "Thanks, guys."

Marty grinned at her. "I've never seen you turn red before."

"My face reddens a lot, because I embarrass easily," she replied. "That's why I wear so much white powder."

Marty held the badge in his hand, admiring it. "Again, you did a fantastic job."

"Definitely," Adam said.

"Thanks," Lynn said, still looking away. "I was afraid you wouldn't like them."

"Are you kidding?" Dee said. "These are amazing and it gives me an idea. That is, provided you enjoyed making them."

"Oh, designing them was fun. What do you have in mind?" Lynn asked.

"You could make badges that we have to earn or to commemorate our investigative accomplishments," Dee said. "Like one for the beating heart mystery in the cemetery. Maybe like a heart underneath a creepy tombstone?"

"Oh!" Adam said. His eyes widened. "That'd be so cool."

"Sounds like fun," Lynn said. "But I'd like *your* help with the artwork. Once we have a pattern, the machine pretty much does the job on its own."

"You bet! This is awesome, guys," Dee said. "Our club's coming together quite well now. After we find Sara's silver bell and get Edgar back, our next goal will be to find ourselves a secret clubhouse. Right now, we need to get to the library."

"No. I need to go home and shower first," Lynn said. "I'm all sweaty, and I stink."

Marty chuckled. "We probably all do," Marty said. "We should shower and get cleaned up. The library doesn't open for another hour."

Dee checked the time on her cellphone. "You're right. We got up awfully early. In all this excitement, I practically forgot the time."

Adam looked at his grimy hands and held his palms toward her. "It'll take a lot of soap and scrubbing for me to forget."

Marty laughed. "If you think this morning was bad, you should try cutting okra, which is almost like touching a cactus each time you get a pod."

"No, thanks. I'm good," Adam said, shaking his head. He hopped on his BMX. "Race you back home."

. . .

A HALF HOUR LATER, the four Mystery Solvers met outside the Sullivan garage on their bikes. A gentle breeze rustled the leaves of the towering oaks that lined both sides of the street. The wind stirred the humid heat without lessening its thick oppressiveness. A brief scent of cocoa butter drifted from the yellowish-white flowers on the tall hedges lining the drive.

Lynn's white face almost glowed from the thick layer of fresh powder she had applied to her face. Her dark hair was brushed neatly and pulled back into a ponytail. Her dark eyes were outlined with black mascara. With her white shirt, shorts, and tennis shoes, she resembled a mime without the black stripes barring her clothes.

Dee wore tan sandals, light green shorts, and a tank top that matched. She also wore a lime green sun visor to block the morning sun on their ride to the library at the middle of town.

Adam and Marty wore cargo shorts and white tank tops. Marty had pinned his Mystery Solvers' badge to his shirt with a safety pin.

"You wore your badge?" Lynn asked, flattered.

Marty shrugged. "Sure, why not? It's our official emblem."

"I need to sew mine to my shirt," Lynn said.

"I'll ask my mother to do that for me later, but I want to pick a shirt that's comfortable regardless of the weather," Marty said.

Lynn smiled. "Once you find the shirt you want, I'd be happy to sew it on for you."

"Thanks."

Dee pulled her badge from her shorts pocket. "I should've thought to get a safety pin, too."

"I have a couple of extras." Marty opened a Velcro-sealed pocket on his shorts. He pulled out a small plastic box and opened it. Inside were several safety pins, straight pins, a small nail, and a couple of matches. He held the box out for Dee.

Dee took a safety pin, as did Lynn and Adam. They pinned their badges to their shirts.

"We *have* to sew these on later today," Dee said.

The sweltering heat rose in visible streams off the blacktop. The sticky air was thick, and they were covered with sweat.

"Let's get to the library," Dee said, "before we melt."

"I bet it's already ninety degrees," Marty said, pedaling ahead of them.

"Why don't we buy ice cream *before* we go to the library?" Lynn asked.

"I'd rather go to the pool to cool off," Adam said.

"Both sound good. Or Sylvan's Cove!" Lynn suggested. "I imagine those places will be packed today as hot as it is."

With a frown, Marty huffed and pedaled ahead of them. Once he was a half a block ahead of them, Dee said, "A gentle reminder. Getting Edgar back for Marty is our first priority. He's right. It's my fault Edgar's in the swamp because I insisted we investigate Tangled Forest. So please, let's concentrate on any clues that help us find that silver bell, if it can be found at all."

"Sorry. I was trying to keep my mind off the heat," Lynn said. "I wasn't being serious about ice cream and swimming this early in the day."

"Me, either," Adam said.

"I know," Dee said, "but Marty's heartbroken about Edgar."

Lynn's eyes moistened. She glanced sadly at Marty. "I love Edgar, too. It's so strange without him appearing each time we stop somewhere."

Adam nodded. "We're going to find that bell today to end the curse."

"We're going to try our hardest," Dee said, pedaling faster.

Marty chained his bike to the bike rack outside the library and headed up the concrete steps to the double glass doors. Two ravens were perched on the power line that connected to the library. The birds craned their necks to the side and made gurgling croaks while watching them.

"Wait up!" Dee said. She, Lynn, and Adam chained their bikes to the rack and hurried up the steps.

Marty pulled open the door and held it. "You sure you guys

wouldn't rather be elsewhere? Like swimming or eating ice cream? Or are you going to take this seriously?"

"Marty, I'm sorry. We want to get Edgar back," Lynn said. "He's more important. I was thinking out loud to get my mind off the heat. That's all. I wasn't serious about doing those things right now. Honest. Besides, the library has air conditioning, which is excellent for today, and even better. I can't get sunburned in it."

Marty stared at her for a few moments and his frown softened. He smiled. "Thanks. You know, I'm surprised you didn't get sunburned yesterday."

"Me, too, but I don't have to worry about that today." She smiled.

Adam shook his head. "I don't know, Lynn. You're pretty pale. So pale those fluorescent lights might actually burn you."

"Hey!" Lynn half-frowned. She turned and playfully jabbed him with an elbow.

After the other three entered the library, Marty stepped inside and let the door close. The air was frosty compared to the sweltering heat outside. Goosebumps pimpled Lynn's and Dee's arms. They visibly shivered and rubbed their arms vigorously with their hands.

"Where should we start our research first?" Lynn asked.

Marty said, "Much of our town's history is well known, even Reverend Chavies. They dedicated placards and monuments to him in reverence. We need to find any secrets about him that no one alive today knows about. Dark secrets were easier kept hidden centuries ago, so the library's archives would be the best place to begin looking."

CHAPTER 13

Most libraries seem shrouded in serenity due to the mutual quietness maintained by the often unspoken rule to not disturb one's neighbor while mentally absorbing the knowledge contained in books, magazines, and newspapers. Indeed this library was soothing in its atmosphere whenever the Mystery Solvers ventured inside to check out books, but that was on the lower levels. The archives, however, were kept at the top floor in what had once been designed as the watchtower of the building.

When Ravenswood first relocated, the courthouse was the tallest building in the town. The roof and upper narrow windows were guarded with armed sentries and watchmen. Over time, outside threats lessened and the need for watchmen became unnecessary. The old narrow windows were sealed with red bricks. After a new courthouse was built, they town declared the old courthouse as the library.

The Mystery Solvers left the main floor and walked up the old creaky wooden stairs. The tranquil mood changed. The stale musty air became colder. Apprehension built between the young detectives.

"Getting kinda creepy up here," Lynn whispered.

Adam gulped. "Yeah, like maybe we shouldn't be going to the top floor?"

Marty paused at the turn in the stairs and faced them. "It's because we've never been to the top floor before."

Dee chuckled. "No one ever comes up here."

"Oh, I'm sure some do," Marty said softly.

"*I've* never seen anyone take these stairs," Dee replied.

"Me, either," Lynn said with a worried expression.

Adam glanced down the stairs. "Look, if we're going to do this, let's get it over with. I'm having second thoughts about seeing what's at the top of the stairs."

Marty shook his head. "Just old books, photos, and documents. If that scares you, perhaps you should never read books again or set foot in a library."

"It's not the books I'm worried about," Adam said.

"Phht! Perhaps you're in the wrong club," Marty said.

"Hey," Adam said. "Don't say that."

"Don't be mean," Dee said with a slight frown.

Marty stared at Dee and then at Adam. "I'm not being mean. He's already seen one ghost. To solve this case, we must find the silver bell. Our best bet is to look at old photos or in journals to find its location." Marty turned and headed up the next flight of steps. "But Adam's right."

Adam looked confused.

"About what exactly?" Dee asked.

"About us getting this over with, so I can get Edgar back," Marty replied. "Come on."

CHAPTER 14

*S*helves of books composed the walls of the top floor. No windows offered light. The majority of the books rested behind glass to prevent dust from collecting on them. Oddly enough, the room was small, roughly eight foot by eight foot, which hardly gave them enough room to stand inside together.

The spines of the hardbound books were rigid with prominent letters embroidered on them.

"Wow," Dee said in an astonished whisper. "These books are crazy old."

"You're not kidding," Adam said. "Are the bookcases locked?"

Lynn eased a glass door open, slipped a book from its shelf, and carefully looked inside. "Nope."

Marty peered over her shoulder at the aged faded pages. "I could spend days reading through all these books."

Lynn looked up at him and smiled slightly. "Me, too."

Adam read some of the spine titles aloud, "*The Founders of Ravenswood, Raven Curse, The Floods of Ravenswood, Swamp Water Rising, Mystical Creatures in the Night, Flora and Fauna of Ravenswood, Midnight Nightmares, The Epidemic of 1822, Witches Amongst Us ...*"

"Sounds like we're not the only ones who have noticed all these strange things," Dee said.

"Yeah." Marty grabbed a thin book next to the one Lynn was studying and flipped it open. *"Choking Out the Evil* … The witch hangings of 1820. Here's the opening: 'Thanks be to Reverend Luther Chavies for ridding our town of devastating evil that lived within our presence. Without his in-depth knowledge of those practicing the occult, the flooding swamps would have swallowed Ravenswood in the Tangled Forest and no one would have survived. For it takes one pure of heart to discern the cursed ones from the righteous."

"That's a sack of stinking manure," Dee said. "I doubt we'll find anything in these books to dispute his *pristine* reputation."

Marty sighed. "I know. Since Reverend Chavies was highly regarded by Ravenswood's founders, even now, us finding any incriminating evidence of his true nature and wrong doings might be impossible to obtain. But even those highly revered have enemies who know the truth. We'll have to dig deeper to find it."

"If what Sara said is true and those hanged with her weren't witches," Adam said, "why'd the people think he was a hero? The others he had killed were innocent."

Lynn placed her book back on the shelf. "Sara said he was a witch, too, and a horribly, evil man guilty of murder. How'd he keep the townspeople deceived?"

"Magic?" Adam asked.

Marty closed his book, shelved it, and reached for another one on a higher shelf. "Possibly, but he could've been an overly charming person. People with excessive charisma can be dangerously deceptive and convince others of their purity while performing the worst atrocities in plain sight."

"So we're probably looking in the wrong place?" Dee glanced at each book title without opening a glass case to retrieve one.

"We should spend a couple of hours searching through the titles. If anything unusual catches your eye, we need to at least scan through the book," Marty said. "But Dee's probably right. Most books left out for people to read have a slanted approval of Reverend Chavies. What we need is a clue about someone who didn't like him at all. If we find such a person, we might be able to research the individual and find more information."

"Sounds good," Dee replied.

Marty glanced at Adam. "Does the room seem scary to you?"

Adam shook his head. "Not at all."

"You see? You were making it out worse than it actually is."

"I suppose."

A loud crack echoed outside. The building shook and the lights dimmed.

"Was that thunder?" Dee asked, looking around.

"I think so," Marty said.

Heavy rain pelleted the rooftop.

"Scratch what I said earlier," Adam said. "That might be a warning that we shouldn't be here."

"Don't be silly," Lynn said with a teasing grin. "Now, we can take our time browsing these books."

"How's that?" Adam asked.

"What can we do outside in a storm?" she replied. "If I'm going to get stuck in a downpour with lightning, I'd rather be inside a library where I don't have to worry about the storm or getting bored."

"But what if the power goes out?" Adam asked.

"We'll be in the dark," Marty said with a broad grin.

Lynn giggled.

"And that doesn't bother you?" Adam asked.

"Not as much as seeing ghosts does."

Dee gave him an odd side-glance. "You don't see any right now, do you?"

Marty shook his head. "Nothing yet."

"Good," Adam said, softly.

Another fierce rumble echoed overhead. The building shook again.

"You think we should go downstairs?" Lynn asked. "That lightning's really close."

"Maybe we should," Marty said. "We can't checkout books in the archives, so each of us should pick two and we'll go down to the next floor and find a table to sit and read."

"G-g-good idea." Adam hurriedly picked two volumes to take with him and headed to the stairs.

"Got mine," Lynn said.

Marty grabbed two old books from the top shelf while Dee chose two at eye level. The lights flickered. They carefully walked down the narrow creaky stairs as quickly and safely as possible. At the bottom of the stairs, the floor was brighter due to the windows.

A glance outside revealed the heavy rain forming puddles along the edge of the road and in the parking lot. Marty eyed the sky through the glass and sighed. "That doesn't look like it will let up any time soon."

Lynn stood beside him and shook her head. "Nope."

A bolt of yellow lightning streaked the sky and struck a tree at the other end of the parking lot. Thunder cracked loudly with a fierce BOOM! The top of the tree burst into flames and dropped onto the power lines. A second later, the library lights went out.

CHAPTER 15

*L*ynn shrieked and leaned against Marty. After her shrill faded, the library was quieter than normal. Air stopped flowing through the ducts. The buzz from the overhead lights silenced. The Mystery Solvers held their breath and exchanged startled glances in the faint lighting.

Dee swallowed hard and after several moments, she whispered, "I never thought a library could be this quiet. The silence seems amplified and my ears are ringing."

"It's way too quiet," Marty said.

"Especially during summer," Lynn said.

Marty sat at a table near the window. Lynn took the seat beside him. Adam and Dee sat at a small table next to the other window. They set their books before them and carefully flipped them open.

A few minutes passed. The librarian's heels clicked across the tile floor with a nerve-wracking echo. Her silver-brown hair was rolled into a tight, neat bun, but her smooth complexion betrayed her age. Her pantsuit and jacket were perfectly creased. She stopped at the window beside the table where Marty and Lynn sat. Grabbing the two metal levers, she turned them downward and pulled the window inward.

"With the power out, it's going to get hot inside if I don't open some of these windows," the librarian said in her stately pleasant tone.

"Do we need to leave, Ms. Cooper?" Marty asked.

Heavy rain poured outside.

"No, I wouldn't ask anyone to leave in this nasty weather. I'm just trying to get the air circulating until the power returns."

"Thanks," Lynn said.

Ms. Cooper paused and glanced at their books on the table. "Are those books from the archives upstairs?"

"Yes," Marty said. "Is it okay that we brought them down?"

"Sure. Just don't get them mixed in with the other return books. Tell me, what are you looking for?" she asked.

Marty closed his book. "We're trying to find out more about Reverend Luther Chavies."

"Ah, I see. The town's founder. Why exactly?" She adjusted her glasses.

He shrugged. "Curiosity mostly, and to determine if maybe people's view of him might be more prestigious than maybe it ought to be."

"Interesting." Ms. Cooper pursed her lips. She offered an amused smile. "Why would you question that? You think the history books incorrectly recorded his legacy?"

Marty thought for a moment. "I don't think *that* necessarily. I understand his prominence, being the town's founder and all, but surely he had some flaws? Some enemies?"

"I'm sure he did. Most people with Chavies' stature tend to accumulate resentment from envious folks, even if they've never done anything wrong. But none were outspoken that I know of," she replied. "And I've read almost every book in the archives."

"Wow," Adam said.

"He had witches hanged," Marty said.

Ms. Cooper nodded. "That's correct."

"But how do we know if they were real witches?" Dee asked.

Ms. Cooper looked unsettled. "What do you mean?"

"History teaches us that most of the Salem witches were innocent people falsely accused over property rights," Lynn said.

Dee, Ms. Cooper, and Marty all gave her an odd glance.

"What?" Lynn said in regard to their stares. "I went to Salem last year with my mother on vacation. We took tours. But if those people were falsely accused, isn't it possible these women might have been innocent of their charges, too?"

"That kind of information might be difficult to find," Ms. Cooper said.

"I agree. And I doubt we're going to find anything negatively reported about him after all these years," Marty said. "Too much time has elapsed."

Ms. Cooper smiled. "You're probably right about that. At least in all the books in the archives. But we do have a collection of artifacts in the basement from the time period when Reverend Chavies was still alive. I believe some of these items were once his property."

"Really?" Dee asked.

Ms. Cooper nodded.

"The library has a basement?" Lynn asked.

"Yes."

"I never knew that," Adam said. "How about you, Marty?"

Marty shook his head. "Nope."

"Could we look at those artifacts?" Dee asked, rising from her seat.

"I'm sorry but it's not currently open to the public," Ms. Cooper replied.

"Aww," Dee and Lynn groaned at the same time.

"Please, could you make an exception for us?" Dee asked.

Ms. Cooper thought for a moment before slightly shaking her head. "I'm afraid with this storm and the power outage that this wouldn't be a good time. Are you doing some type of research project for school or is this strictly self-interest?"

"Kinda both," Dee replied.

"What do you mean?" Ms. Cooper asked.

"Well, school's out but who knows what our teachers might assign when the school year begins," Dee said with a broad grin.

Ms. Cooper smiled. "I suppose that's true. We're trying to contain a mold problem in the basement. Once it's under control we hope to open it to the public. We have several dehumidifiers down there but for some odd reason, nothing seems to stop the moisture from seeping through the concrete walls."

"Why keep the artifacts down there?" Marty asked. "Couldn't the constant moisture damage them?"

"It would if the objects weren't packed in airtight containers."

"When the power comes on, could you show us the basement?" Dee asked.

Ms. Cooper bit her lower lip for a moment. "Only if … no, not today. I have other things I must attend to, but maybe we can schedule a time later in the week. It'd have to be after hours though."

Lynn frowned. "Why?"

"Until we're ready to make the room available for the public to view, we need to keep it secret. So please don't tell others about where we store the artifacts. Once the moisture's under control, we'll hire a security company to set up an alarm system with motion detectors and cameras. A few items in our collection have quite a bit of value, so that's another reason not to advertise the items in our possession."

"We won't tell." Dee pointed at her club badge. "We're great at keeping secrets. That's why we've formed our own club."

Ms. Cooper rested her hands on her hips. She leaned closer to read the club's name. "Dee's Mystery Solvers? Ah, yes, you're the ones who went to the cemetery last year, right?"

"Yes, ma'am," Dee said with a bit of triumph in her voice.

"Well, you're certainly braver than I. I wouldn't ever go in a cemetery after dark, especially not on Halloween night. Please, excuse me. Someone's at the desk and want to check out some books. I imagine they're in a hurry to get home before this storm gets any worse." Ms. Cooper smiled. "And when you're done with those books, please leave them with me at the desk."

"Sure thing," Marty said.

After the clicking of her heels faded into the other room, Dee whispered, "We need to get in the basement to see if that bell is with the other artifacts."

"And then what?" Marty asked. "You plan on stealing it?"

"No-o-o. Just borrow it."

"In order to borrow something, you need to ask permission first," Marty said. "Otherwise, it's stealing."

"We don't even know if it's there. And if it is, I doubt she'd allow us to borrow it. Besides, don't you want to know what's down there?"

"Of course I do," Marty said.

"So do I," Adam said.

Lynn nodded. "Me, too."

Dee sat down and looked around. "Where do you think the door is? I've never noticed one."

Marty shook his head. "Come to think of it, neither have I, and we've been all through the library."

"Then it's hidden," Dee said in a whisper. "It has to be."

"But why?" Lynn asked.

"That's part of the mystery," Dee said with a grin.

Marty shook his head and rolled his eyes.

A flash of lightning brightened the room for a moment, followed by a heavy rumble of thunder. A warm breeze flowed through the window and rattled the metal blinds.

"Dee, don't get ahead of yourself," Marty said.

"You want Edgar back, don't you?"

"Of course I do." Marty frowned.

"Then we must check out everything."

"How do you propose we do that in broad daylight with the librarian watching us?" Marty asked.

"Genius!" Dee whispered sternly.

"What?"

"We come back tonight and look for it," Dee said.

"You mean break into the library?" Adam asked. His brow furrowed. "Like with ski masks and black clothes?"

"No," Dee said with a stern frown.

"Dee—" Marty said.

"I'm not saying we break in to anything," she replied.

"Then how else would we look for the bell?" Lynn asked.

"Maybe the door to the basement is on the outside of the building?" Dee asked.

"It's still breaking and entering," Marty said.

"Do you want Edgar back?"

"You know I do, but I don't want put in jail or to become a juvenile delinquent in order to get my cat. We're not going to have that type of club."

"No, silly," Dee said.

Heavy rain thrummed the rooftop and flowed off the roof in waves, splashing loudly on the paved parking lot.

Marty shook his head. "No. I agreed to go to the swamp only to make certain none of you got hurt. That wasn't voluntary but something I had to do. But we're not going to wander around the streets at night like a bunch of thieves. It's not the reputation you want."

Dee sighed. "Papaw already told me never to get on the wrong side of the law, and I promised not to."

"Good," Marty said. "Then there's no sense continuing this discussion."

"But if you'd just listen for a moment—"

Marty flipped his book open and scanned a page with his finger, obviously ignoring her.

"What's that?" Lynn reached for the edge of Marty's book.

"What?" he asked.

"Look." Lynn tugged at the corner of back page and the loose paper slid.

"Don't do that," Marty said. "You're going to tear the book."

"I don't think it's part of the book," Lynn said softly. She tugged a little more and smiled. "See? This paper's different."

Marty carefully turned the book to the inside back cover. The yellowed paper Lynn had pulled had been placed in between the hard cover and the paper lining. Someone had probably hidden it many years before.

"You're right," Marty said. He helped Lynn carefully slide out the folded yellow parchment.

Dee hurried to the table. "Open it."

The four Mystery Solvers leaned over the table as Marty gently unfolded the paper.

"Oh, my gosh! It's a map," Adam said.

"Shh!" Dee glared at him. She turned the map toward herself. Her eyes scanned the paper quickly. She glanced at the others. "What place does this map represent?"

Marty turned his head to the side so the map appeared upright to him. "Looks like underground tunnels, Sis."

"Wow," Adam said. "Here in Ravenswood?"

Marty shrugged. "That'd be my guess."

"Cool," Adam whispered. "I didn't know there were tunnels under Ravenswood."

"None of us did," Marty replied.

Lynn placed her finger at the bottom left corner at the fancy scrolled letters in faded ink. "Look, someone's name."

"Josephine Abbott," Dee whispered. "I wonder who she was?"

"I don't know," Marty whispered. "But it's one big clue."

"I agree," Dee replied. "Exactly what was this map made for?"

"That's hard to say."

The four studied the map.

"There's an asterisk near what looks like a possible building," Dee said.

"It's hard to make any sense of this map though," Marty said. "A lot of these buildings, which *aren't* identified on the map, are no longer standing. Some were torn down and new ones constructed before we were born. And even if there were names, I imagine a lot of the names have changed, too."

Ms. Cooper's heels clicked across the tiles. The echo indicated she was headed in their direction.

Dee took the map and refolded it. She tucked it into the pocket of her shorts.

"What are you doing? You can't take that," Marty said. "It belongs to the library."

"It's not part of the book. Someone hid it there," Dee said. "So, technically it's not stealing."

"*Technically*, it doesn't belong to us."

Lynn sat back in her chair. "Maybe not, but we might need it."

Marty gave his sister a stern look. "Dee, please give that—"

"How's the research coming?" Ms. Cooper asked, crossing the room to their table.

"Good!" Adam blurted. He quickly jerked his head in her direction.

"Did I frighten you?" she asked. "Surely you heard my shoes."

Marty shook his head. "He's scared of thunderstorms, Ms. Cooper. That's all."

"No, I'm not!"

A bright flash of lightning burst downward with explosive thunder grumbling and shaking the ground. Adam visibly jumped in his seat.

Dee and Lynn giggled.

"Okay," Adam said, shaking his head. "Maybe a little. This storm has been bad."

"I agree," Ms. Cooper said, walking to the open window. A strong wind blew into the room carrying large drops of rain. "This is brutal weather and seldom something we see in Ravenswood. The last time … we had that nasty flood."

"That flood was on this side of town, too." Lynn's eyes widened.

Ms. Cooper turned toward them and bit her lower lip. "The water's starting to stand outside. Let's hope this stops soon or we'll be trapped."

CHAPTER 16

*M*arty stared out the window at the dark swirling clouds. Sheets of raindrops spiraled with the sharp breeze. The howling wind splashed water across the windowsill. The rainwater dripped on the floor and formed a puddle. Ms. Cooper hurried and shut the window.

A few moments later the lights flickered and the power hummed before the fluorescent lights beamed brightly in a harsh steady glow. A rush of air flowed from the vents overhead with a loud *Whoosh!*

The Mystery Solvers cheered.

Ms. Cooper sighed, turned, and adjusted her glasses. "That's a relief."

"What? The power coming back on?" Dee asked.

She nodded. "We need the air conditioning more than the lights right now. Excuse me, I need to close the other windows."

"We can help you close them." Marty stood.

"Sure," Dee said. "Right, Lynn?"

Lynn nodded.

Ms. Cooper smiled. "That's very nice of you. I appreciate your help. I'll close the ones on the other side of the library, while you close the ones in this room and those surrounding the circulation desk."

She hurried through the door with solid click-clacks of her shoes steadily fading.

"While we close the windows," Dee said, "look for an inconspicuous door. One we've apparently overlooked every time we've been in the library."

"On it," Adam said with a sharp nod.

Marty walked into the large circular room where the librarian's information desk set in its center. Four curved desks were positioned to form a large oval. Glancing around, he realized the large library was empty except for the librarian and the four club members. Dee and Lynn headed between the reference shelves toward the smaller windows at the opposite end of the library.

No one sat at the computers or in the lounge where a large window offered a panoramic view of the city park across the street. Plush recliners set in different corners where patrons could read and relax, and most of this floor was covered by new carpet from a recent donation given to the library.

Wind rustled announcement flyers taped to the main glass door, so Marty hurried to a small window in the corner above an old filing cabinet. As he pushed the window down, he noticed a painting of an old Victorian mansion. Beneath the house in tiny print was: "Josephine Abbott's Estate." Recognizing the name from the map, he was stunned, so he leaned closer.

"Beautiful, isn't it?" Ms. Cooper asked.

Marty jumped and spun toward her.

"Sorry," she said, "I didn't mean to startle you."

"I didn't hear you approach."

"That's what I like about this new carpet." She smiled. "It softens the sound of these loud shoes. It's kind of hard for me to shush others when I make more noise walking than they do whispering."

Marty chuckled and returned his attention to the picture. "I don't recall seeing this mansion ever."

"That's because it burned down."

"When?"

"Over a hundred years ago."

"Oh," Marty said.

"You sound disappointed," Ms. Cooper said.

"It's a shame the place is gone. It was a beautiful building."

"It was. A lot of the historic buildings burned during that time period all across our country. Back then they didn't have much of a fire department or access to water, other than wells. It was nearly impossible to put out a fire once it started."

"Who was Josephine Abbott?" he asked.

Ms. Cooper stared at the painting and shook her head. "That's something else we've lost in time."

"What do you mean?"

Ms. Cooper cupped her hands together at her waist and offered a slight shrug, while studying the painting. "Obviously, she was a person of wealth and importance since she lived in such an estate, but no records other than the painting of this house remain. She's been forgotten by time."

Marty frowned. "You mean there's no written record of Josephine in Ravenswood? Not even at the cemetery?"

She shook her head. "No, she must have been buried elsewhere."

"What about Ravenswood's other cemetery?"

"Other cemetery?" Her head jerked, and she peered into his eyes. "Are you talking about the one in Tangled Forest?"

Realizing he had given more information than he intended, he took a step back and tried to hide his nervousness.

"You've been there?" she asked.

He cleared his throat. "I've heard about the cemetery from my grandparents, along with all the other scary things that have occurred out there. Have you heard about it?"

Ms. Cooper studied his face for several seconds. "I've heard about the cemetery, too. I've never had the courage to go see for myself, of course. I'm not the adventurous type, and I value my life. But, you know, in spite of the haunted tales about those woods, someone should explore that cemetery."

"Why?"

"None of the people buried there were ever registered in

Ravenswood's new settlement records. We've no recorded history of them. It'd be nice to know what contributions they might've offered in the original settlement. It's truly a shame they've been forgotten."

"None of them are in the town founders' records?"

"No."

Marty shook his head and looked at his feet. "Have you ever wondered why the graves were abandoned?"

"I'm a history buff," she replied. "So, yes, from time to time I wonder about what occurred in that forest so many years ago. Why? Do you have an opinion?"

Marty sighed and dared to look into her eyes. "I'm not sure, of course, since it was so long ago, but like I mentioned before, nothing negative's ever been written about Reverend Chavies. Well, at least nothing's been found yet, but it's odd how the township moved abruptly."

"Are you insinuating that Reverend Chavies sentenced innocent people to be hanged as witches?"

"What if they weren't really witches?" he asked with a slight shrug. "Such murders occurred in Salem and in England."

Ms. Cooper took a sharp breath and held it.

"What's wrong?" he asked.

She rubbed her arms. "I just got a chill."

Marty felt the sudden coldness brush past him, too. He glanced around and expected to see a ghost staring at them. He was relieved that one wasn't nearby.

"What you're proposing about Reverend Chavies are severe charges against a man held in high esteem," she said.

"I know. I'm not trying to tarnish his reputation."

"A century ago, such allegations could've resulted in the person being ostracized by the town. Two centuries ago, one could've been severely punished or killed."

Marty swallowed hard. "That's my point though."

She studied him with curiosity. "About the witches?"

"Yes. With the severity of the punishment for even questioning the

Reverend's motives, who'd dare stand in defense of the falsely accused?"

Ms. Cooper smiled. "You definitely use your critical thinking skills to analyze all the possibilities. Most teenagers nowadays are obsessed with texting and technology."

"I read a lot, and I visit the library all the time."

"I know. The four of you come in here all the time. But today's the first time I've seen you take a keen interest in the Archive books and the subject of Reverend Chavies. Why the sudden interest?"

"Curiosity, I suppose."

Ms. Cooper gave a sideways grin.

"What?" Marty asked with feigned innocence.

"I'm beginning to think that you've been in the Tangled Forest."

"Where was this estate?" Marty nodded at the painting and quickly changed the subject.

"The city park across the street. Where her house was, is now covered with large oaks."

A ray of sunlight broke through the sky. Soft thunder rumbled in the distance. Ms. Cooper smiled. "Looks like the storm has passed."

"Good." Marty glanced at the main door.

"That's great!" Dee rushed to where Marty and Ms. Cooper stood. Lynn and Adam followed close behind. "We closed all the windows in the Reference section. Now, can you show us those artifacts?"

Ms. Cooper opened her mouth to reply but the sound of slamming car doors echoed outside the library and caught her attention.

Several elderly people were walking up the sidewalk to the main door. She glanced at her watch. "Oh, I'm sorry. It's almost noon and time for the book club meeting. Since the storm's breaking up, I guess people are finally venturing out. I need to fill the coffee decanters and set out cookies. Sorry."

Dee couldn't hide her disappointment, but she kept her silence.

"Perhaps in the near future," Ms. Cooper said. "Okay?"

"What about tonight?" Dee asked. "Doesn't the library close at six?"

"It does, but unfortunately I have an obligation out of town."

"I see." Dee nodded and glanced at the door. "Looks like you're going to get busy."

"Yes," Ms. Cooper agreed. "And please remember not to mention the artifacts. We're still months away before we can present them to the public."

"We won't tell anyone. I promise." Dee grabbed Marty's elbow and tugged. "We should go."

Marty looked at Ms. Cooper. "Thanks for your help."

"Any time," she replied.

"Yes, thank you," Lynn said.

Dee hurried to the main door and after an elderly gentleman and his wife stepped through, Dee darted outside.

CHAPTER 17

A few seconds later the Mystery Solvers stood outside the library in the sweltering heat. The thick air was difficult to breathe. Under the harsh sun, the rain rose like steam. Water dripped from the buildings, trees, and trickled in heavy streams from the drainpipes. Water flowed along the side street like a stream, carrying leaves, cigarette butts, and other debris along with it.

About a dozen more people slowly made their way across the parking lot toward the library's main entrance.

Marty smiled and nodded at the people walking past him.

Lynn fanned her face with her hand. "Sheesh, it seems hotter now than before."

"It's the humidity, young lady," an elderly man said as he closed his car door and smiled. "That's the worst part of a brief shower on an extremely hot day. It gets muggier and stickier. Best find yourselves a place with a nice air conditioner and keep cool. It won't get any cooler out here until after dark."

He shuffled past them and steadied himself with his bent cane.

"Why are you in such a hurry to leave the library, Dee?" Marty asked.

"I thought we all had agreed," she replied.

"On what?"

"That we weren't going to find anything negative in those books about Reverend Chavies and Ravenswood."

"We probably won't," Marty said.

"Besides," she said, glancing at each of them. "Did anyone find a door to the basement?"

They all shook their heads.

"So we don't have anything really to go on," Dee said. "Maybe we should return to the swamp so you can talk to Sara?"

Marty shook his head.

"Why not?" Dee frowned with frustration.

"Come with me." Marty turned and waved his hand for them to follow. "I found a clue."

"Really?" Dee asked. "What?"

"What'd you find?" Lynn asked.

"It could be something helpful but it might not be, so don't get your hopes up yet," Marty said.

"What about our bikes?" Adam yelled.

"We don't need them right yet. It's within walking distance."

Marty jogged several yards along the sidewalk and paused to look both ways before sprinting across the street. His shoes splashed through the receding water as he ran. He stopped on the other side of the street and waited for the rest of the group.

"Walking distance?" Adam yelled. "Then why are you running?"

Marty laughed.

"The city park?" Dee said. "Why?"

Water dripped from the tree limbs and leaves, making soft blooping sounds in the widening puddles. A couple of squirrels crept slowly down the side of a tree. They seemed to study the wet grass with a sense of dread.

"Remember the name on the map you took?" Marty asked.

"Josephine Abbott?"

"Yes. That painting Ms. Cooper and I were looking at right before people started arriving … Well, that mansion belonged to Josephine,"

Marty said. "Ms. Cooper said her house once stood somewhere in this park."

"For real?" Lynn asked.

"That's what she told me. But, she also said nothing else is really known about Josephine. I suppose if it weren't for the painting of her mansion, she'd be forgotten all together."

"That's sad," Lynn said softly.

Dee frowned. "If that's true, how'd the painting survive?"

"Another mystery, I suppose," Marty said.

"I *thrive* on mysteries!" Dee replied.

Adam shook his head. "Well, there's nothing but trees and park benches now. So what are we supposed to do?"

"What we're supposed to do in this club. We look for clues," Dee said.

"Dee," Marty said. "Can you show us the map?"

"Sure." She reached into her pocket and slipped the folded yellow parchment out. Carefully, she opened it.

Marty ran a finger down the map to the spot where the mark had been drawn. "It's hard to distinguish what these tunnels represent, but for starters, let's suppose she put the mark to represent her home. So, if that's the case, this is the center spot and we might be able to figure out what the map leads to."

"If it leads to anything at all," Dee said.

"Think about it, Sis. Josephine was wealthy. Her house burns down and she's no longer remembered? She's erased? Just like all those tombstones in the swamp. The townspeople were forced to leave the old township, but isn't it odd that no one moved the graves to the new graveyard? Why would their remains be left in the swamp to be forgotten?"

Lynn's eyebrows rose. "That is odd."

"Do you think Reverend Chavies forbade people from going back to the graveyard to pay their respects?" Dee asked.

"I'm not certain," Marty said. "But it seems that way."

"But why?" Adam said.

"They were accused of being witches," Dee said. "So the Reverend cursed them. I'd guess no one chose to return to memorialize them because they feared they'd be accused of the same thing."

Marty pointed. "That's an excellent point. Maybe Josephine went against what the Reverend commanded and he set her house on fire? And according to Ms. Cooper, Josephine's not buried at the cemetery in the new Ravenswood."

"Then what happened to her?" Adam asked.

"That's what we need to find out," Marty said.

"I thought we're looking for the bell?" Lynn said.

"We are," Marty said. "But I wonder if the two things are somehow related."

Water flowed loudly near the downward slope of the city park. The bottom of the old slanted trench was layered with centuries-old bricks and reinforced with new concrete, which captured the water. The trench was approximately two feet wide and two feet deep. Its steep angle caused the runoff to rush downhill like a rapid stream. The rushing water gushed through a square brick grated drain.

"Wow," Adam said, looking at Marty. "Did you know this was here?"

Marty nodded. "I used to set some of my Hotwheels cars at the top of the hill and watch them race to the bottom."

"Did you lose them in the drain?"

Marty shook his head. "No. I placed a tree branch to prevent them from going over into the drain. But I've never seen it filled with water before."

Dee crouched and looked down the drain. "That sounds like a long ways down. Where do you think that goes?"

"The sewers would be my guess," Marty said.

"Maybe it flows out into Burnside Creek?" Lynn said.

Marty and Dee exchanged glances.

"Could be," Dee said. "This trench is very old and probably here before the mansion burned. So where do you think the foundation of the mansion might've been?"

Marty looked around at the tallest oak trees. "It's hard to predict which side of the trench it would've stood. I'd think after it burned, all the stones of the foundation would've been hauled away. There's no evidence a house was ever here."

"Um, guys," Adam said. "Didn't Ms. Cooper say that she needed to get things set up for the book club meeting?"

"Yes, why?" Dee asked.

Adam pointed across the street at the library. "Isn't that her watching us through the lounge window?"

All of them turned their attention to the library. Ms. Cooper stood with her arms crossed, intently watching them.

"She doesn't look happy," Lynn said.

"Yeah, but we're not doing anything wrong," Dee said.

Marty nodded. "You're holding the map."

"She can't tell from that distance what it is or where we found it." Dee slowly refolded the map.

"Maybe not," Marty replied. "She doesn't appear mad. Only curious, but from this distance, it's hard to tell."

Dee folded the map. "Let's get our bikes and ride to Burnside Creek to see if this water drains into the creek. I don't think we'll find anything useful in the park."

"Sounds good to me," Adam said.

Marty sighed. "For what reason, Dee? We're supposed to be looking for clues to get Edgar back. Even if this spills out into the creek, what good will that do us? We have a better chance of finding something in the park."

"In broad daylight?" Dee shook her head. "We can't dig in the park, just like we cannot break into the library to hunt for the hidden doorway."

"You're right on both accounts, so what good is going to the creek?" Marty asked.

"The map shows a tunnel system. The running water in the park is going somewhere. None of us can fit through the grate covering the drain. Even if we could, the fall would probably kill us. But, if this water comes out at the creek, we might find a larger tunnel that leads to the underground tunnels."

Marty thought about her argument for several seconds. He grinned. "That's the best idea you've presented concerning this case."

"Thanks," Dee said with a broad smile.

"But it doesn't excuse the fact that I don't have Edgar since I had to go to the forest to watch out for all of you."

Dee's smile faded. "I'm truly sorry about that. Okay? That's why I'm willing to search anywhere to help you get Sara's bell so she can break the spell. Once she does, you'll have Edgar again. It's my way of taking responsibility. Okay?"

Marty stared at her. Tears tugged at the edges of Dee's eyes. Her cheeks flushed red. If he didn't say something, he knew she was going to cry.

He released a reluctant sigh. "I appreciate that. I do. I'm sorry for bringing it back up, but I'm frustrated. I'm afraid I've lost Edgar for good. So, let's get our bikes and go. The longer we stand in the park, the more suspicion we're going to draw upon ourselves."

"But before we head to the creek, can we do something first?" Dee asked.

Marty glanced toward her. "What's that?"

"Let's ride around the outside of the library and search for a door to the basement. If we don't find one, we know the only way into the basement is on the inside."

"Still thinking about breaking in, huh?" Adam said with a sly grin.

"No-o-o. But it'd be nice to know where the door is since we can't find one inside the library," she replied.

"Fine, but let's be inconspicuous," Marty said. "Ms. Cooper's already watching us."

CHAPTER 18

*A*fter a quick bike ride around the library, the Mystery Solvers didn't find any doors other than the main door and one emergency side door. None seemed to lead to a lower level, so they rode to the street.

Fifteen minutes later, they stopped at the bridge that crossed Burnside Creek and looked off the edge. Due to the heavy rain, the creek was swollen to the edge of its banks.

"The water's up," Marty said.

Dee nodded. "Yep. The good thing about all the rain is no one's fishing today."

"Probably not," Adam said. "Nothing should be biting in that muddy water."

"Catfish might," Marty said. "Doubtful anyone's willing to get soaked to catch them."

Lynn stared at the turgid brown water with disgust. "No way I'm wading in that."

Dee pushed her bike off the road and down the narrow, worn path made by those who fish beneath the bridge.

"Where are you going, Sis?"

"We can't see much from up here."

"You want to walk along the creek *now*?" Lynn looked at her shoes and shook her head.

"No time like the present," Dee replied.

Lynn cringed. "There's always time to get an older pair of shoes. These are my good ones."

"Then take them off," Dee said.

Lynn shook her head. "No way I'm walking barefoot through the sticky mud or in that brown water."

"Dee, the creek's too high to think about looking for a possible drainage culvert," Marty said.

Lynn looked slightly relieved.

"We'll be fine as long as we're careful," Dee said.

Adam chuckled. "It's only water."

"And mud!" Lynn said with disgust. "I'm not taking off my shoes and getting squishy mud between my toes! You know there are leeches in creeks, right?"

Dee sighed. "At least you're not wearing hightop sneakers. My mom's going to kill me for getting them wet."

"My mom will kill me if I muddy up *these* shoes," Lynn said.

"Dee, we should wait," Marty said.

"No," she replied. "We need to find the bell. The sooner, the better. You want Edgar. We all do."

"He'll be okay for another day."

"Will you?"

"It won't be easy, but yes, I'll survive," Marty replied.

Sadness came to Lynn's eyes. "Marty, I'm sorry."

"No, Lynn's, it's okay. I promise." Marty smiled at her. "Let's do the diplomatic thing and take a vote. How many want to wait until tomorrow after the creek's gone down?"

He, Adam, and Lynn raised their hands. Dee looked defiant, her jaw tightened, and her eyes heated with tears.

"This is mutiny!" she said.

"No, Sis, this is strictly for safety reasons. None of us are prepared to wade a creek. We dressed to do research at the library. Now, I make a proposal that we do what Papaw said to do. We treat ourselves to some ice cream."

Adam adjusted his ball cap. "Yeah. I'm for that."

Lynn smiled. "Me, too."

Dee took a deep breath and slowly exhaled.

"Rocky Road, Sis?"

A gentle smile tugged at her lips. "I suppose you're right. Okay."

Marty gave a nod. "We can get a booth and look over this map while we eat and figure out how to prepare for tomorrow."

CHAPTER 19

*T*he ice cream shop was frigid compared to the hot and humid atmosphere outside. They each bought a cone with two scoops of ice cream and sat a booth near the window that gave them the best view of the public library.

Marty scooted against the wall and Lynn sat beside him. They faced Adam and Dee on the other side of the table.

"I don't get it," Dee said.

"What?" Marty asked.

"We never found a door leading to the library's basement."

"You're not going to let that go?" Marty asked before licking his ice cream.

"Ms. Cooper got my curiosity up. That's all. I mean, why bring it up in the first place, if all she's going to do is tease me with the information?"

Lynn shrugged. "I think she wanted to take us down there, but she seemed hesitant to do so."

"Yep." Adam turned his ball cap around backwards. "I kinda thought she was going to take us before all those people started showing up."

"Yeah, but she still acts like she's hiding something," Dee said.

Marty nodded. "She knows a lot more than she's telling us."

"Why do you say that?" Lynn turned slightly to face him.

"When she and I were looking at the painting, she knew a lot about Josephine, even though she says not much is written about her."

"Well," Adam said, "she *is* a history buff. She's probably read all the books in the Archives. Maybe there are bits of information about Josephine in those books, but you'd have to read all the books to piece it together?"

"We don't have time to do that," Dee said.

"I agree," Marty said.

"I know, but that's possibly *how* she knows." Adam hunched forward, propped on his elbows, and licked a trickle of melting ice cream off the side of his cone.

Dee gave Marty a stern look. "We should go talk to Sara again."

Marty shook his head. "No. I don't want to return to Tangled Forest until we find Sara's bell. That way, when we're in there, we let her undo the spell, and we're out. We never need to return."

The metal bells jingled on the ice cream shop's door. Two of their teen classmates entered.

"Perhaps we should talk to Ms. Cooper about this?" Adam said.

"Shh!" Dee said, giving him a firm stare. "It's Caleb and Brooke."

"So?" Adam said.

Dee frowned. "Although it's not a written rule in our club, we should keep all our club discussions private."

"They can't hear us," Adam said.

"All the same." Dee rolled her eyes. "Great. Brooke's coming over here."

Brooke Summers was in Dee, Lynn, and Adam's classes. Marty was two grades ahead of them. Tall, slender, with brown hair and brown eyes, she cocked a brow at them as she walked to their table. She often acted haughty during school and snubbed Dee and Lynn, so Dee was surprised Brooke even bothered to notice them.

"Hey!" Brooke said in a high tone. "What'cha all doing in here?"

Lynn rolled her eyes.

Dee frowned slightly. "Eating ice cream. You?"

"Caleb and I are picking up our order and taking George and Julie their milkshakes at the gym," Brooke said.

"The gym?" Adam said.

Brooke grinned at him. "Yeah, the big building behind the school where the basketball court and goals are."

Adam's jaw tightened. "I know *what* the gym is. Why this time of the summer?"

"Yes. I'm sure," Brooke replied. "He and George have football practice in a while since the storm finally ended. Julie and I have cheer practice."

Lynn scoffed. "What a way to spend your summer."

"I'm sure it beats whatever you guys are doing," Brooke replied. She noticed the patch on Dee's shirt. "Oh? What's this? D's Mystery Solvers. Hmm? What's that mean?"

"We have a club," Adam said.

Dee glared at him.

"A club? Oh, fancy that," Brooke said, touching the patch slightly with a condescending smile and batting eyelashes. "That's cute. Something like Scooby Doo?"

Lynn's face reddened enough it was visible through her pale makeup. Her hands balled into fists under the table.

"No," Marty said. "Just something we do to have fun."

Without shifting her gaze from the patch, Brooke said, "How'd you get these patches?"

"Lynn made them," Dee said.

"Ah, I see," Brooke said. "I thought maybe from a cereal box."

Lynn stiffened and looked ready to charge across the table, but Marty gently wrapped his hand around her wrist. He slightly shook his head.

"Brooke!" Caleb said, raising his carryout tray with four milkshakes up. "Let's go!"

"Catch ya guys later," Brooke said. She turned quickly and her brown ponytail swished in the air.

The Mystery Solvers all exchanged angered stares and watched Brooke and Caleb walk across the street.

CHAPTER 20

"I never liked Brooke," Dee said, fuming.

Lynn huffed. "I like her even less than before. Though, I never paid her any mind. A cereal box? Really?"

"She's just jealous," Dee said.

"Of what?" Lynn asked. "I don't understand why she made it a point to even come to our table. She never socializes with any of us during the school year."

"For one," Dee said, "these badges you made. She could never make anything with equal the quality of what you did."

Lynn blushed. "She'd be jealous of me and the badges? Really?"

Marty nodded. "Yes. You could see it in her eyes. Don't let it get to you. The patches are fabulous and I wear mine with pride."

"Me, too," Adam said. "She thinks she's better than the rest of us. And Caleb's a jock who likes to tease me."

"Since when?" Marty asked, perturbed.

Adam shrugged. "Whenever we pass in the halls."

"What's he tease you about?" Marty straightened in his seat.

"How short I am. Every now and then, he—" Adam cleared his throat. "He grabs my ball cap and tosses it back and forth with his buddies, just out of my reach."

Marty nodded. His jaw tightened. "If he does it again, let me know."

"It's not that big a deal," Adam said.

Marty pointed to his club badge. "You're in our club. I won't have him bullying you."

"I don't want you to fight him and get into trouble," Adam said.

Marty shook his head. "I won't fight him. I don't need to, but him worrying about the possibility might intimidate him enough to leave you alone."

"Jocks and cheerleaders," Lynn said with a sigh. "The stuff we nerds have to deal with. Like ignoring them isn't enough. You'd think Brooke could find better things to do than be insulting and condescending to me."

Dee nodded. "Right. For now, let's set her remarks aside and return to what we were discussing about Ms. Cooper."

"Are you suggesting I tell her about Sara, the cat, and the bell?" Marty asked.

"You said she knows more than she's telling us. Maybe she'd tell us more if we let her know what's going on?"

"Oh, she knows a lot more. She had difficulty holding back what she wanted to say. I understand. But I'm not about to tell my secret to anyone else. I had a hard enough time telling all of you. But Ms. Cooper implied that most everything about Josephine was lost over time," Marty said. "And insinuated that she knows I've been in Tangled Forest."

Their eyes widened.

"Why do you think that?" Dee asked.

"I kinda let it slip."

"You *told* her?" Dee frowned.

"No, I hinted I had been there, but quickly corrected myself. However, what I said afterwards didn't lessen her suspicion. She went on to say that she wished someone would explore and investigate those swamps."

"Why?" Lynn asked.

Adam leaned back against his seat and folded his hands behind his head. "Yeah, why?"

"She's heard of the graveyard in the swamp.None of the people buried there are even in the historical records of the new Ravenswood settlement," Marty replied.

"That's awful," Lynn said. "To be forgotten."

"It is," Marty agreed.

Dee's eyes widened, and she pointed a stern finger. "Yes! I knew it." Marty and Lynn flinched.

"What?" Marty asked with a confused grin.

"I told your ability to see ghosts—"

"Shh!" Marty shook his head. "Keep your voice down."

"Sorry." Dee's face reddened. "Anyway, your ability could help ghosts resolve wrongs from the past. Did you see a lot of ghosts when we were out there?"

"A dozen or so," Marty replied.

"What if Edgar lured you there, not only to help Sara, but to ensure all the others were properly buried like they deserve?" Dee asked. "Maybe that's why so many restless spirits remain active in the swamp?"

Adam pounded his fist on the table with a solid thud. "No wonder you're our club leader with these kind of thoughts."

Dee grinned and her face heated an even deeper red. "Thanks, but it's just a thought."

"Wow, Sis. I never thought about that. Perhaps you're right. I never considered anything positive about seeing ghosts, especially after one attacked me. So, Tangled Forest isn't just about helping Sara and getting Edgar back. It's much broader. A lot of those graves are sinking. How many might've already sunk? This is far more important than Sara's bell."

"But we still need the bell, right?" Lynn asked.

"Of course," Marty said. "We have to break the binding spell on Sara and get Edgar back."

"Do you think if we were able to get the graves moved into

Ravenswood cemetery that Tangled Forest would no longer be haunted?" Adam asked.

"I can't really say," Marty replied. "We'd only know afterwards."

"Hmm." Dee tapped a finger on the tabletop. "Should we meet early in the morning to return to the creek?"

"Sure," Marty replied. "I'm not certain what you hope to find if the drain empties into the creek, but we can look."

Lynn and Adam nodded.

"Before we totally settle on that," Dee said, "let's ride back to the bridge and look at the creek before heading home."

"Dee—" Marty said.

"No, I don't plan to go into the water or even to the creek bank. I want to look from the center of the bridge toward the city park. There might not be any reason to go tomorrow."

"As long as that's the only reason," Marty said.

"It is. I promise."

CHAPTER 21

*S*ince the traffic on the road that crossed Burnside Creek was always sparse, the four Mystery Solvers stopped riding their bikes midway across the narrow one-lane bridge. The brown water continued flowing rapidly and was slightly above the creek's banks. The sun had faded behind thick gray clouds that hinted of more rain.

Balancing his bike while straddling it, Marty watched the water. "Well, are you satisfied?"

Dee nodded. "I suppose so. I don't see anything—"

Re-ee-oww!

"It's Edgar!" Dee pointed.

"You see him?" Marty asked.

"I heard him," Adam said.

Lynn perked up and looked over the side of the bridge. "Me, too."

"He's right there," Dee said.

Marty frowned and squinted. "I don't see him."

"Look at the sharp bend of the creek," Dee replied. "He's right at the edge of the bank, but almost out of sight."

"Yeah." Marty smiled. His chest swelled with relief. "I see him now."

Marty got off his bike and pushed it to the other side of the bridge. "You guys stay here. I'm going to get him."

"Not a chance," Dee said. "I'm going with you."

Marty guided his bike down the narrow muddy trail and balanced his bike against a small sweetgum tree. Dee set hers beside his while Adam and Lynn placed theirs against another small tree.

"You guys stay with the bikes," Marty said. He jogged down the narrow trail that ran between the creek and a pasture. He didn't need to look over his shoulder to tell the others were running behind him. Their shoes smacked on the muddy bank.

Before he could say anything, Dee said, "No arguments. We all want Edgar back."

As they came closer to Edgar, the cat scampered farther away from them on the bank and meowed as he ran.

"Where's he going?" Adam asked.

"I think he wants us to follow him," Marty replied.

Dee panted. "I agree."

Once they ran past the sharp bend in the creek, a small row of trees lined the bank. The rushing water became louder.

Marty looked over his shoulder and frowned. "This creek's too small for a waterfall."

"Maybe it's the runoff from the park," Dee said.

"Possibly."

On the other side of the sapling row, the creek widened with an eroded sandbar on their side. About four feet over the creek was a large rusted pipe encased in bricks. Water gushed from the pipe and spilled into the creek with the sound of a small, cascading waterfall.

"Look," Dee said in a near whisper.

Under the pipe was a rotted piece of sheathing board. It was propped upright with a sagging 2 x 4. Near the bottom was a small opening. Edgar glanced at them for a moment, meowed, and darted through the hole.

Marty hurried to the board. "Everyone stand back."

"What are you going to do?" Adam asked.

Marty kicked the 2 x 4 loose. The rotted sheathing board collapsed into several pieces. Behind the board was a narrow arched tunnel with bricked walls and ceiling. Edgar meowed and darted farther into the tunnel.

"Edgar!" Marty said in a scolding whisper.

Several of the ceiling bricks were on the tunnel floor, which indicated the possible danger of a cave-in should they proceed to follow the cat. Marty slid his cellphone from his back pocket and scrolled until he found his flashlight app. He clicked on the bright light and shone it in the direction the cat had run.

"You're not going in there, are you?" Adam asked.

Marty sighed. "I don't want to, but Edgar led us to this tunnel for a reason. No one has to follow me, but I want to know why he wants me to follow."

Dee smiled broadly. "This *must* lead to the underground tunnels."

"We'll soon find out," Marty said.

"Are you sure he wants you to follow him?" Adam asked.

"His cries are exactly the same way when he called me to find him into the swamp. Apparently there's something for us to find. Otherwise, he'd have stayed with Sara. Besides, he's never ran away from me when I've called for him."

Lynn knelt and untied her shoes.

"Lynn, you don't have to go inside," Marty said.

Lynn slipped her shoes and socks off, tied the laces together, and slung them over her left shoulder. When her toes sunk in the gooey mud, she looked at Marty and smiled. "For me to be doing this, I hope you know how much I like you."

Marty blushed and looked into her eyes.

Embarrassed by her admission, she averted her gaze and cleared her throat. "So we can get Edgar for you, I mean."

If she was blushing, he couldn't tell due to her makeup but her sudden shyness indicated she probably was.

Re-e-ow! echoed farther inside the dark tunnel.

Marty smiled at Lynn before turning and stepping over several bricks. With the tunnel only about four feet in height, he hunched and placed his left hand against the wall to keep his balance as he walked.

"You … you don't think there's bears or wildcats in here, do you?" Adam asked.

"Bears?" Marty chuckled. "You think a bear would close the makeshift door behind him?"

"Good point," Adam said. "All the same, a bear could use this for a den."

"Nah," Marty said. "Edgar isn't worried about wild animals. Besides, there hasn't been a bear reported in Ravenswood for years."

"But the cat has one advantage we don't have."

"What's that?"

"He can disappear whenever he wishes."

"Yeah, but he'd never lead us into danger," Marty replied.

Water droplets splashed on his face and the floor. Marty paused and looked over his shoulder. Lynn stood behind him, turned on her flashlight app, and held the light over the spot before her. Mud covered her feet, but she didn't protest, despite the disgusted expression on her face.

Dee was behind her with her light, and Adam stood behind her with his.

"We're all here," Dee said. "What are you waiting for?"

"Be careful where you step. The floor's uneven in places, and as you probably see, bricks have fallen from the ceiling, so we need to be cautious. More could fall at any time, so let's pray the ceiling doesn't collapse."

"Marty," Lynn said. "Should we turn back? It's bad enough I have to worry where I step in this slimy water without having to worry about falling bricks or smacking my forehead against the ceiling."

"All I'm saying is we should be cautious. I don't expect a cave-in, but it's always possible." Marty turned and stared ahead. Edgar's green eyes reflected in their lights for a moment. Then the cat darted off.

The four staggered awkwardly for about ten yards. Several times Marty contemplated turning back, and each time, Edgar poked his head out and meowed. Gradually, the ceiling became higher and the floor smoother.

"Well, this is an improvement," Dee said. "I can finally stand upright."

"The mud's gone, too," Lynn said, relieved.

Marty turned toward them. "We must be under Ravenswood, now."

"The tunnels," Dee said. "I was right!"

Her voice echoed.

"Yep," Marty said. "Now the big question is, 'where are we exactly?'"

"Maybe the park?" Adam said.

"It depends on how many tunnels intersect," Marty said.

"Do you see Edgar?" Dee asked.

Re-e-ow!

"On cue," Adam said with a nervous laugh.

Marty held his light in the direction of Edgar's mew. The cat scampered out of sight. "Come on. He's not far. Looks like he took a side tunnel."

"I hope he knows where he's going," Adam said.

"A cat with his own GPS system built in," Dee said.

Marty laughed.

Lynn held her light higher to join with Marty's light to brighten the path. "At least we're not walking in the sewers."

"That's a plus," Dee said.

"Why would these tunnels be here in the first place?" Lynn asked. "What purpose do they serve?"

"A lot of the older towns and cities have underground passages," Marty said. "I think sometimes they were dug so people could hide during attacks or emergencies. As time went by, they were sealed off and forgotten."

Re-ee-ow!

"Where is he?" Dee asked.

Green eyes glowed.

"There!" Lynn said.

The four Mystery Solvers rushed toward the cat, but when the reached the spot where he had been, Edgar vanished. They stood at intersecting tunnels.

"Which way should we go?" Dee asked.

Marty looked each direction. "Whichever direction we choose, we need to be certain that we mark the wall so we don't get lost."

"Here," Adam said.

"What?"

Adam handed him a piece of a white rock he had found on the floor. "Maybe this can help?"

Marty scraped the rock against the left corner. The rock was like a piece of chalk and left a broad white stroke on the wall. "Good. Okay, we go left first. I think that'll take us to where the city park is."

"Where's Edgar?" Dee asked.

"He vanished, but he'll return soon, I'm sure. Come on." Marty led the way.

They walked about fifteen yards, and Edgar's eyes gleamed in the beams of their lights. The little cat squeezed through a crack in the wall before they reached him.

Marty groaned with frustration.

"Is Edgar always like this?" Adam asked.

"No," Marty replied. "He must have something he wants us to find."

Dee took her cellphone flashlight and held it closer to the crack and tried to see inside. "What could possibly be in there?"

"Step back for a moment," Marty said. After she moved back, he pulled at the edge of the wall and tore loose a piece of plaster. "That's odd."

"What?" Dee asked.

"Someone must've constructed a fake wall a long time ago," he replied. He gripped another piece of the plaster, which was fastened to a board. After it dislodged, a huge section of the fake wall dropped, causing the Mystery Solvers to back away a few steps. The plaster and pieces of rotted lumber crashed to the floor and shattered.

"It's a hidden room." Dee stepped closer and shone her light. The others joined her, adding more light into the room. "What's all of this stuff?"

"That's an altar," Lynn said, pointing. "Looks like it was used for incantations."

Marty and Dee gave her an odd look.

"Remember, I told you that I went to Salem," Lynn said softly.

"About that," Dee said, "you never told me anything except you went to Boston."

"Yes, but you can take a train from Boston to Salem. That's what my mother and I did. We spent the entire day exploring all the shops, museums, and the graveyards. That's why I recognize this as a witch's hidden altar room."

"They teach that kind of stuff in Salem?" Adam asked.

"Sure," Lynn replied. "They sell all kinds of supplies, too."

"Can you explain what's here?" Marty asked.

Lynn stepped closer to the small table. "Candles are obvious, right? There's a chalice, a offering bowl, a crystal, and that book possibly is a spell book."

"There are more books over here," Dee said. She picked up one and wiped off a layer of dust. She flipped it open and held her light above it. "A journal."

"Who's journal?" Marty asked.

"Josephine's."

"Look, guys," Lynn said. "A silver bell."

Adam stepped closer. "Could it be Reverend Chavies' bell?"

"Doubtful," Marty said.

"Actually," Dee said, "It might be."

"How do you know that?" Marty asked.

"Listen to this entry," Dee said.

CHAPTER 22

"*Six weeks have passed since Sara Wolcott was accused and hanged for being a witch. My desire to exact vengeance has not lessened, despite the repercussions that would befall me for cursing the man who falsely identifies himself as 'Reverend'.*

Chavies betrayed us, those who practice the craft and follow the ways of nature, and Ravenswood. His betrayal is far worse since he sought to kill those he has partaken with, those he secretly identified himself a part of, and for the murders he committed. He did these atrocities for profit and to magnify his esteemed reputation amongst those who have no idea how black his rotted soul actually is.

For him to sever my sisterly bond with Sara has drawn me closer to madness and enhanced my cause to exact justice for the helpless. At the same time, I'm wary that I might become his next victim.

But what Chavies doesn't realize is how I continue to communicate with Sara. Her death didn't break our bond of love and magic, but instead, it opened a new realm of understanding I never knew existed. For after her death, I can still see her, at least her image, but only at the place where she was hanged. I wonder if our connection remains because of my familiar, Pyewackett. She's only visible when my black cat accompanies me.

Sara revealed to me the horrific curse the 'Reverend' added to her death.

He cast a binding spell on her, so she'd never find rest in the world beyond. She's forever fastened to the unhallowed ground where she'd died at the end of a rope, and for as long as he lived, he'd taunt her.

Sara told me her silver bell was the only way to break Chavies' spell. He used the bell to bind her. Her bell I now possess, for I sneaked into his home and stole it off his altar. Although no one witnessed my theft, I remain his chief suspect. He will come for me, to kill me, and should he succeed before I release Sara's spirit, the 'Reverend' will set into motion a curse to infest and destroy Ravenswood. If I should die at his hands, nature will respond in kind by swallowing the town in stagnant water. Ravenswood will suffer an unkind fate for Chavies' evil deeds."

Dee stopped reading and looked at the others. "Do you realize what this means?"

"A lot of things," Marty replied. "What's your take on it, Sis?"

"For one, Edgar or *Pyewackett*, belonged to Josephine. He's the reason she could see ghosts like you. So the reason Ravenswood had to be moved was because Josephine cursed the original settlement if Reverend Chavies killed her before she set Sara free."

"He killed her?" Adam asked.

Dee nodded. "He must have. Sara's ghost is still at the church. The swamp is swallowing the cemetery and the old church. No one knows exactly what happened to Josephine. So Chavies must have killed her, too."

"That's sad," Lynn said.

"Then this bell is Sara's?" Marty asked.

"I believe so," Dee replied.

Marty picked up the bell. As soon as he touched it, a harsh wind flowed through the outside tunnel and rushed into the room.

"Anybody else feel that?" Adam asked with wide eyes.

"Yes," Lynn said.

"What was it and what should we do?" Adam asked.

"We need to find our way back to the surface," Marty replied.

"I'm for that." Lynn's nervous eyes gazed at the narrow opening.

"Let's go," Marty said.

Dee looked at her brother. "You don't see any ghosts down here?"

"No. Not yet."

"Hmm, I wonder what became of Josephine?" Dee asked.

"It's not what we should worry about at the moment," Marty said. "When I grabbed the bell, I set something in motion."

"What do you mean?" Adam asked.

"Someone or something is looking for the bell. I don't know anything about witchcraft, but I wonder if there's a locator spell on it. The second I touched it, the wind entered. It's not a coincidence." Marty took the silver bell, placed it inside a large pocket of his cargo shorts, and pressed the Velcro edge secure.

"I don't think it is, either," Dee said.

Marty nodded at the narrow opening. "Let's find Edgar and get out of here."

The four Mystery Solvers squeezed through the crack in the wall and stood in the tunnel.

"Which way should we go?" Dee asked.

Marty sighed. "Edgar led us in here. I was kinda hoping he'd show us the fastest way out."

Adam gave a nervous laugh. "It'd be our luck that he stays invisible now."

Re-ee-ow! Edgar's green eyes peered at the intersecting tunnels for a moment before it darted down a path.

"Come on," Marty said.

They rushed to the intersection with their cellphone lights shining brightly.

"Where'd he go?" Dee asked.

"There!" Marty pointed. "He's standing at the corner near a door."

"A door?" Dee stepped around Lynn to stand beside Marty. "Wonder where that leads?"

Lynn said, "Well, I hope it leads to another way out. I don't want to walk through that slimy muck again."

"Agreed," Adam said.

"Before we go any closer," Dee said, "Marty, do you seen any ghosts in the tunnels?"

Marty shook his head. "I haven't yet."

"That's good," Adam said.

"Yep. So far, so good," Marty replied. He approached the door and reached for the doorknob. His heart pounded in his chest. His voice shook. "Brace yourselves and be prepared to run."

Marty turned the doorknob, closed his eyes, and pulled the door toward him. After a second or two, he opened them, and was prepared to run. A small set of stairs led up to a level platform.

At the center of the room was a glass-covered table with various odd and end items that looked antique. Dee held her light over the table and scanned the items. Marty found an old door on the other side of the room. He tried to turn the doorknob, but the door was locked.

"You think these are the artifacts Ms. Cooper mentioned?" Dee asked. "Is this the basement?"

Marty shrugged. "Could be."

"Phht," Dee said. "Really? What a ripoff. She made it sound like she had a lot of things down here. And there doesn't seem to be any moisture or mold problems in this room."

"Shh!" Adam said.

"What?" Dee whispered.

"Listen, someone's coming," he replied.

The clicking sound echoed overhead for a moment. A few seconds later, the rusted hinges whined.

"Someone's opening a door," Lynn whispered and hugged herself.

"It's not the one in front of us." Marty held the light so they could watch the doorknob, should someone turn it.

"I suggest we run back out the way we came," Adam said.

A key turned in the lock. A harsh click echoed. Before the door opened, overhead lights brightened the room. After the door swung inward, Ms. Cooper stood in the doorway with her arms crossed. She shook her head and tapped her foot. "My, what do we have here?"

CHAPTER 23

*M*arty swallowed hard and took a few steps back to get closer to Dee and the others. At the same time, he kept himself between them and the librarian. If she chose to attack, she'd have to deal with him first.

Ms. Cooper uncrossed her arms, took her cellphone, and ran her finger across the screen. "Dee, I'm disappointed in you. I promised to show you this room but you lack the patience for a more convenient time? I expected better."

"No, Ma'am," Dee said.

"This is breaking and entry, though I'm surprised you found another way to enter this room." Ms. Cooper frowned. "All this time, I thought you were wonderful teenagers who had a knack for learning."

"We do," Marty said.

"This is unlawful." Her finger tapped the screen of her phone. "I'm sorry, but I'm afraid I have no other choice but to call the police and report your trespassing."

"Please, Ms. Cooper—" Dee said.

"Unless—"

"What?" Adam said.

"Unless you come clean. What are you looking for and did you plan to *steal* it from the library?" she asked sternly, without the slightest hint of a smile. Her voice was icy, unlike any time she'd spoken to them before.

"We found what we needed," Dee said. "But not in this room. In one of the other tunnels. We were only trying to find another way out when we happened into this room. Honest."

Ms. Cooper studied Dee for a few moments. She tucked her phone into her skirt pocket. "May I see what you've found?"

"We'd rather not, Ms. Cooper," Marty said. "Not yet, at least."

"And why not?"

"It's personal and well, a secret," he replied.

"A secret?" Her jaw tightened. She took her phone from her pocket again. "Then we'll let the authorities sort this out."

"No," Dee said, with pleading eyes. "Please."

Marty shook his head and reached to unfasten his pocket.

"No, Marty," Dee said. "It's the only way you'll get Edgar back."

"We can't go to jail over a cat," he said.

"What are you talking about?" Ms. Cooper asked.

"I'll tell you, but you're not going to believe it," Marty said.

"Try me," she said. "I've read a lot of things over the years. There's not much that *surprises* me."

"I can see ghosts," Marty said.

Ms. Cooper's brow furrowed for a moment, then she cocked one brow. "Okay ... I must admit that's *not* what I expected you to say."

"But it's true. Anyways, my cat isn't a normal cat. He's kinda paranormal," Marty said.

"Oh, how?" Ms. Cooper asked.

"See? I knew you wouldn't believe me," Marty said.

"He can vanish and reappear," Dee said.

"Where's your cat right now?" Ms. Cooper asked, looking around.

Dee grinned. "He's around somewhere. I'm sure he'll pop up at any time."

Marty nodded. "Anyway, up until I found Edgar in Tangled Forest, I couldn't see ghosts but after I got him, that's when I started seeing them."

"Tangled Forest," Ms. Cooper said. "I suspected you were lying about not entering the forest."

"Not lying. I chose not to tell you because I'd have to explain all this and you'd think I was crazy, like you probably do right now."

Ms. Cooper laughed softy. A grin spread on her lips. "Now why would I think that? It sounds preposterous, but your club's to solve mysteries, so I suppose you might exaggerate situations to better your need for further investigations. But what have been looking for?"

"A bell that belonged to Reverend Chavies." He yanked the Velcro pocket open and pulled out the bell.

Her eyes widened. "Where'd you find that?"

"A hidden room down one of the tunnels," Marty replied.

Her eyes never left the bell. "Why do you need that?"

"So he can keep Edgar," Dee replied.

"Because of a bell? What's so special about it?" Ms. Cooper stepped closer.

"Like I said, I can see ghosts. Edgar belongs to a ghost in the swamps deep in the forest. The bell belongs to Sara Wolcott. She asked me to bring the bell to her," Marty said.

"Sara Wolcott? She's the ghost?"

Marty and Dee nodded.

"Why does she need the bell?"

Marty glanced toward Dee with a questioning look. Dee nodded. "To set her spirit free. She's stuck between realms by a curse Chavies cast on her. When we talked earlier, I mentioned he might not have been a good man. Anyway, this bell breaks the spell."

"Interesting," Ms. Cooper said. She smiled and reached for the bell. "May I?"

Marty's hand tightened around the bell, and he pulled it to his chest. "Ms. Cooper, I'd rather not. After I set the ghost free, I'll be happy to donate it to this artifact collection, okay?"

"Okay, that sounds great, but on one condition?"

"What's that?"

Ms. Cooper glanced at each of them. "I want to be there when you do the ritual. I assume you must do something like that, right?"

119

"Uh, we're not exactly sure what to do," Marty replied.

"The Tangled Forest is a long way across the county. How'd you plan to get out there?"

"On our bikes, like we did the last time."

"Well, you'd never make it there and back before dark," she said. "How about, since the library's closed, I go home and change into more appropriate clothes for hiking. I'll drive us all out there. Would that be acceptable? It's like we discussed earlier, Marty, someone needs to go and assess the graveyard. I could see the condition of the graves, take pictures with my phone, and make an appeal to the city council to have those graves moved. Would that be okay?"

Marty shrugged. "Sure. That'd be helpful."

Dee nodded. "Yeah, thanks."

"I certainly wasn't looking forward to biking all the way back out there," Adam said, shaking his head.

"Good," Ms. Cooper said. "Let's go upstairs, so I can lock up."

"Thanks. We need to get our bikes, though," Marty said.

"Where are they?"

"At the Burnside Creek bridge."

"I can drop you off there. Get your bikes and return to the outside of the library. You can lock them to the bike rack. I'll swing by to pick you up in about forty-five minutes. Okay?"

"Sure," Dee said. "That gives us enough time to get better shoes from the house and let our parents know."

Ms. Cooper held open the main library door until the Mystery Solvers exited. Then she shut the door and locked it. She pointed. "That's my car. Hop in and I'll take you to the bridge. On the way to Tangled Forest, perhaps you can tell me how you found your way into those tunnels?"

"Okay."

AFTER RIDING to their houses and changing into hiking clothes, Dee's Mystery Solvers returned to the library. Ms. Cooper was parked near the bike rack and smiled as they rode into the parking lot. They chained their bikes to the rack.

Marty got into the front passenger seat, while the other three squeezed into the backseat and buckled their seat belts.

Ms. Cooper wore blue jeans, a denim shirt, and a hat. Marty doubted he would've even recognized her had he passed her in public. She was dressed so contrary to her normal business-like apparel.

Ms. Cooper glanced into the rearview mirror and smiled. "Everyone ready?"

Adam, Dee, and Lynn all nodded.

"Great."

By car, the trip was faster than Marty imagined. They passed Ol' Henry's General Store, and Marty was glad to be in the car and not on his bike. The cool air conditioning was much better than the horrid heat they'd have suffered riding across country on their bikes. His hand rested on the bell hidden in his pocket. While there was the possibility the bell might not be the right one, he believed the odds were far greater in their favor that it was.

Ms. Cooper asked a lot of questions about the bell, how they found the tunnel system, and she asked more about the ghosts Marty had seen. Her interest was genuine and her demeanor lightened after they agreed to let her witness the ritual. He imagined her brief anger was simply from the surprise of finding them in the library without permission, which by his own admission was illegal entry. He could see any business owner rush to the conclusion of possible theft. For what other reason should anyone be inside a room or building that's locked and off limits to others?

Ms. Cooper parked her car at the graveled bend at the edge of the road outside Tangled Forest. Marty nervously opened his door and got out. The others got out, too, and shut their doors softly.

"How far is it?" Ms. Cooper asked, adjusting her hat.

"Several hundred yards," Marty said. "Since we pretty much

cleared a path the last time, it shouldn't take us near as long to get to the church in the swamp."

Re-ee-ow!

Ms. Cooper's shoulders tensed, and she jerked slightly.

"Edgar?" Dee rushed across the gravels and knelt to pet Edgar.

"This is your cat?" Ms. Cooper asked.

Marty nodded.

"How'd he get all the way out here?"

"That's what I've been trying to tell you. It's just something he does."

Ms. Cooper frowned. "So he really was in the tunnels with your earlier?"

"Yes," Marty replied.

"And now, he's here?"

"Yes."

Ms. Cooper shook her head. "Wow. Simply amazing. Okay, I have my phone, so who wants to lead?"

"I will," Marty said.

CHAPTER 24

*I*n less than twenty minutes Dee's Mystery Solvers and Ms. Cooper stood at the edge of the swampy water near the church.

"Here we are," Marty said.

Ms. Cooper used her phone camera to snap several pictures of the sinking tombstones. "Wow. This place is in worse shape than I imagined. There's no telling how many graves are already under water."

"I know," Marty replied.

"I'm surprised the church is still standing," Ms. Cooper said.

Marty nodded, glanced at the church, and smiled.

"She's there?" Dee asked.

Marty nodded.

"Who's where?" Ms. Cooper asked, frowning.

"Sara Wolcott," Marty replied.

"Sara Wolcott? I don't see her."

Dee grinned. "None of the rest of us do, either."

Marty reached into his pocket for the silver bell while he smiled at Sara. "I found it."

Sorrow came to Sara's eyes. "How could you betray me like this?"

"What do you mean?" Marty asked.

"What's wrong?" Dee asked.

"I'm not sure," he replied. "What's troubling you, Sara? How have I betrayed you?"

"You brought Reverend Chavies to destroy me!" Sara shrieked.

"What?" Marty asked.

"Give me the bell, boy!" the voice said behind him.

Marty turned. The man's voice came through Ms. Cooper. Her eyes were yellow and a man's face shimmered over the librarian's.

"He's come to destroy me for good!" Sara wailed.

"How?" Marty asked.

"Ms. Cooper?" Dee grabbed her arm.

Ms. Cooper gripped Dee's arm and flung her into the shallow swamp water. "Give me the bell, boy, or all of you perish in this swamp!"

Marty's eyes widened. He ducked as Ms. Cooper rushed and tried to envelope her arms around him.

Re-ee-ow!

Edgar sat atop the tilted angel tombstone. His green eyes blazed. Static filled the air. Wind rustled the trees that surrounded the church and graveyard.

The cat jumped from the tombstone, scurried across the narrow flow of swamp water, and hissed. In seconds, the cat was between Marty and Ms. Cooper.

Dee sat up in the water and glanced at Lynn and Adam. "Are you guys seeing this?"

They nodded. Sara's image became visible as did Reverend Chavies' face covering Ms. Cooper's.

Ms. Cooper pointed a stern finger at Marty. "Give me the bell or it's your death." The possessed librarian's hand rose. Bluish fire blazed from her fingertips.

Edgar flung himself into the air with claws widened and slashed Ms. Cooper's arm. When the cat landed on the soft mossy ground, a figure shot out of the cat and slowly materialized into another female form.

This figure glanced toward Marty. "You must get the bell to the small circle drawn about Sara's spirit. Ring the bell thirteen times within the circle. It's the only way to free her."

"Josephine?" Sara asked, perplexed.

The ghost smiled at Sara. "I told you I'd find a way to free you."

Marty rushed across the wet ground. His feet sunk in places, but he fought to keep moving. Ms. Cooper came at him with a fiery stare and a deep rumbling voice that made chill bumps run down his spine. He ran faster.

"Today, vengeance is ours," Josephine said to Ms. Cooper. She flung her hands at the librarian. "Reverend Chavies, we banish you! Release this lady you've taken, and may your soul forever suffer in fiery torment!"

Bluish flames swept through the air and encircled the librarian's body. Within seconds, Ms. Cooper dropped to the ground, weeping and hugging herself. Reverend Chavies' spirit stood above her body in his glowing ghostly form.

"You think you've the power to stop me?" His voice thundered. "You're powerless against me."

Marty stood almost toe-to-toe with Sara. He rang the bell with a flick of his wrist.

Wind rushed through the swamp. Light encircled Marty and Sara. Adam and Lynn helped Dee to her feet. They hurried up the small bank to stand with Marty and hugged one another.

Josephine faced the Reverend. "Look around you, Luther. I'm *not* alone."

Ghosts rose from the swampy waters, from the trees, and from the mossy earth in massive numbers. "Time doesn't erase the transgressions you've bestowed against Sara, myself, and all the others. We've waited a long time for you to return."

The angered ghosts formed a tight circle around Chavies.

"No-o-o!" he bellowed.

Marty rang the bell for the thirteenth time. Sara rose from the spot where she had stood for nearly two hundred years. In less than the blink of an eye, she was at Josephine's side. They joined hands and began to chant.

Black smoke rose around the Reverend's feet, a fiery circle formed, and a moment later, his spirit was snatched and pulled under the earth. His horrified scream echoed and faded until no more sound came from him.

Ms. Cooper cowered on the ground, trembling. With fear in her eyes, she peered around. "Wh-what happened?"

Marty and the other Mystery Solvers crossed the narrow water. Josephine and Sara stood before Ms. Cooper. Marty looked at them. "She doesn't know?"

Josephine shook her head. "No. She's innocent of what Chavies did. She played no part in this. She was an unfortunate vessel."

"Will she be okay?" Dee asked.

Josephine nodded. "She'll be fine, once her shock passes."

Marty frowned. "How long has she been possessed?"

"That's difficult to determine," Josephine said, hovering near Ms. Cooper.

The librarian slowly sat up and rubbed her temples. She looked at Marty, but with a blank expression as she spoke. "Marty, do you remember when we were talking about the painting of Josephine's mansion?"

He nodded.

"I got cold chills and felt something icy rush inside me."

"I remember feeling a cold presence while we talked, but only for a moment," Marty said. "I looked around but never saw a ghost." He offered his hand to Ms. Cooper and helped her stand.

She looked around nervously. "Is Reverend Chavies gone?"

Josephine offered an endearing smile. "He's gone for good. He can never bother anyone ever again."

Slowly the ghosts faded from everyone's view, except Marty's.

Ms. Cooper looked around. "Where'd the ghosts go?"

"They're still here," Marty said.

"Please give them my thanks," Ms. Cooper said. "Please tell them I'll solicit the Ravenswood city council to exhume these graves and move them to the new cemetery, which should've been done ages ago."

Sara smiled at Marty. "We'll finally have peace and rest, so we never need to roam again. Speaking for the others, we're eternally grateful for new burials where we'll no longer be forgotten."

Marty relayed the message to Ms. Cooper.

Sara embraced Josephine. "When did you become a part of Pyewackett?"

"Pyewackett was there when Luther dropped me down my well at my estate. After I drown, my spirit found him and he graciously allowed me residence."

"What are they talking about?" Dee asked.

"I'll tell you all later," Marty whispered. He looked at Sara. "All this time you didn't know she was in your cat?"

"No," Sara replied.

Marty reached down and scooped up the cat. "What happens to Pyewackett now? Will he also disappear for good?"

Josephine smiled. "I believe he desires to stay with you."

"Was it your idea for him to call me into the forest to find him?" Marty asked.

"No," she replied. "He understood Sara and my burdens. After nearly two centuries of carrying me and my grief around, such a burden must have wearied him, too. So, not only have Sara and I been freed, he has been, too. We give all of you our blessings. Thank you for having the boldness to pursue this matter until the end. No words adequately express our gratitude."

CHAPTER 25

The following morning Dee called a special club meeting to mark the case as *solved*. Marty made the suggestion to change Edgar's name to his original, Pyewackett, which was agreed by a unanimous vote.

After meeting with the city council a few days later, Ms. Cooper started a petition to have the graves exhumed and moved to the newer cemetery in Ravenswood. Since townsfolk feared Tangled Forest was haunted, the council was also fearful that the residents would protest such a major decision because of their fear that ghosts might terrorize the town. But if she could prove differently, they would take appropriate means to move the graves.

She needed 500 signatures before they'd take further action. Dee's Mystery Solvers volunteered to do the leg work by going door-to-door and soliciting signatures while reassuring the people they had nothing to fear by having the graves moved. When anyone was reluctant to sign, the Mystery Solvers implied that if a teenager wasn't frightened to allow the proper respects to the deceased in the swamp, it'd be shameful for any adult to hold such fear. Getting enough signatures could take several weeks, but they refused to give up. Sara and

Josephine and the dozens of others deserved the Mystery Solvers' devotion to fulfilling their promise. Besides, Pyewackett was quite outspoken whenever he chose to be, and he wouldn't allow them to forget.

THE END

EPILOGUE

*M*s. Cooper sat at a small, pentagram-shaped table in the attic of the library. A black silk cloth covered the table and a smaller silk cloth was draped over a crystal ball. The table was hidden in a nook behind a false bookshelf. Although the Mystery Solvers had been in the archived books small room, none of them discovered the latch to open the door to the nook. Old buildings and houses often had secret doors and passages, much like the underground tunnels in Ravenswood.

Ms. Cooper smiled at Caleb and Brooke who sat on each side of her, while Julie Welsh and George Gordon sat across from them.

Julie was a snooty blonde teenager with blue eyes. Like Brooke, she was a cheerleader but her degrading attitude was worse. She savored and took delight in showing her superiority over those she deemed less important.

George Gordon was lanky with dark hair and beady brown eyes. He stood slightly stooped and was overall a quiet teenager. His buck teeth prominently stood out. Before he spurred sudden height during the previous summer, many of his classmates had teased him about how his facial features and his teeth made him look like a rodent. That was near the end of the school year. But when the fall term started, he stood well over six feet tall. Those who had teased him suddenly feared him. He refused to be the butt of their jokes and no one dared test to see how Gordon might react. He didn't play football with Caleb, but with his increased height, he was asked to play basketball by the coach. He agreed to tryout and made the team.

Ms. Cooper cleared her throat. "So glad you could join me this evening at such short notice."

"You said it was important," Caleb said, combing his red hair with his fingers.

"It is," Ms. Cooper said.

"Oh?" Brooke folded her hands and rested them on her lap. "What's so important?"

"It'll be in tomorrow's newspaper," the librarian said. "But, I'll give you the news ahead of time."

Julie's brow furrowed. "What sort of news, and why does it concern us?"

"Some disturbances have occurred and changes have been made," Ms. Cooper said. "I'm sure you're aware of Dee Sullivan and her brother, Marty. They have a mystery solving club."

Julie smirked. "Yeah, so?"

Brooke laughed. "I saw their cute little badges the other day. You'd think they were in grade school."

Brooke and Julie exchanged glances and burst into laughter.

"Hush!" Ms. Cooper's eyes narrowed.

The girls' laughter ceased and fear claimed their demeanors.

"When I helped initiate the four of you into your own club under my guidance, you swore you'd find the artifacts I demanded. You've found nothing," Ms. Cooper said. "You're the Secret Sleuths, and yet, Dee's Mystery Solvers found several artifacts I needed. Not only that, they've sent Reverend Chavies to the abyss."

George frowned. "How?"

"They searched for clues, *found* the clues, and using proper reasoning, they obtained the silver bell and Sara Wolcott's lost journal. Something you failed to do."

"That doesn't explain *how* they did it." Caleb nervously combed his red hair with his fingers. "How'd they accomplish what we failed to achieve?"

Ms. Cooper winced and sighed. "I can't remember. My mind blanked for several hours."

Julie met Ms. Cooper's nervous gaze. "What happened?"

Ms. Cooper sighed. "The last thing I remember was talking to Marty about the painting in the library. Then, a cold surge entered me. I think it was Chavies' spirit. Whatever was said afterwards, I don't recall. When he was driven out of me and sent to the abyss, I came to my senses. But during the time he controlled me, I've no recollection. Perhaps he wouldn't have possessed me if you had found the silver bell. You failed us. *Me.*"

"We're sorry," Brooke said. "We can do better."

"Somehow, I doubt that," Ms. Cooper said. "Under my guidance with the use of the crystal ball and the Ouija Board to contact Reverend Chavies, you should've found the items long before Dee's Mystery Solvers did. Without my ability to contact Chavies any longer, my power no longer exists."

"What do you want us to do?" Julie asked.

"Disband the club," she replied.

"Disband it?" Caleb said. "That's a bit extreme, isn't it?"

"You didn't devote adequate time to the cause anyway," Ms. Cooper said. "You can abandon it, or—"

"Or what?" Brooke asked.

"You can spy on the Mystery Solvers and report to me what they're doing and whatever they discover."

Julie snorted. "They never associate with us. It's doubtful they'll have anything to do with us and find it suspicious that we'd want to talk to them."

Ms. Cooper shrugged. "Not my concern."

"We'll keep our eyes on them," Caleb said. "Maybe we can unravel what they learned that you can't remember."

Ms. Cooper rubbed her temples. "That'd be wonderful. I've never experienced a memory lapse."

"Of course," Caleb said. "We'll have to wait until after the school year starts. Otherwise, they'll be suspicious of our proposed friendships."

Julie laughed. "They probably will anyway."

Ms. Cooper nodded and offered a faint smile. "That's fine. Plan to meet with me one week after school starts."

The Secret Sleuths nodded. The five reached across the table and clasped hands. In unison, they said, "So be it!"

THE END

ABOUT THE AUTHOR

Leonard D. Hilley II grew up a quiet, shy kid with an inquisitive mind. Learning to read at an early age, he fell in love with books. He read every book he could get his hands on and stacks of dark comics about ghosts, monsters, and creepy things that stalk the night.

Like a lot of boys, he caught beetles, wooly bears, butterflies, and had an ant farm. When he was ten, his interests in science increased even more after seeing a professor's insect collection. Soon he set out on his quest to build his own collection. He also learned to rear butterflies and moths to obtain perfect specimens. He learned botany, gardening, and set his goal to become an entomologist.

At eleven, he saw Star Wars. His imagination soared. Soon after, he discovered Roger Zelazny's Chronicles of Amber. Six months later, he had written the first draft of a novel. A novel he later discarded, but the characters stuck with him. Years later, these characters came to life in Shawndirea, which Hilley intended to be a novella for Devils Den. The characters, however, refused to be ignored and took the opportunity to unveil Aetheaon in their first epic fantasy. Lady Squire: Dawn's Ascension was quick to follow.

Shawndirea was Hilley's farewell to butterfly collecting, and those who have read the novel understand why. He has taken Ray Bradbury's advice to heart: "Follow the characters." He does. He follows, listens, and take notes—often never knowing where they're going to take him, but he's never been disappointed in the results.

Hilley earned a B.S. in Biology and an MFA in Creative Writing to combine his love of science and writing.

Sci-fi Titles: Predators of Darkness: Aftermath, Beyond the Darkness, The Game of Pawns, Death's Valley, The Deimos Virus.

Epic Fantasy: Shawndirea (Aetheaon Chronicles: Book One), Lady Squire (Aetheaon Chronicles: Book Two), Frosthammer (Aetheaon Chronicles: Book Three), Shadowfae (Aetheaon Chronicles: Book Four), and Devils Den.

UF/PR: Succubus: Shadows of the Beast (Nocturnal Trinity Series: Book One), Raven (Nocturnal Trinity Series: Book Two), A Touch of the Familiar (Nocturnal Trinity Series: Book Three)

YA UF/Paranormal: Forrest Wollinsky Vampire Hunter; Forrest Wollinsky: Blood Mists of London; Forrest Wollinsky: Predestined Crossroads.

DEE'S MYSTERY SOLVERS: The Beating Heart Beneath Hollow Hill Cemetery; Witch Cat; Buried Treasure; The Clubhouse